D0783659

The Big Book of
School Stories

The Big Book of
School Stories

Published by the Penguin Group
Penguin Books Ltd, 27 Wrights Lane, London W8 5TZ, England
Penguin Putnam Inc., 375 Hudson Street, New York, New York 10014, USA
Penguin Books Australia Ltd, Ringwood, Victoria, Australia
Penguin Books Canada Ltd, 10 Alcorn Avenue, Toronto, Ontario, Canada M4V 3B2
Penguin Books (NZ) Ltd, Private Bag 102902, NSMC, Auckland, New Zealand

On the World Wide Web at: *www.penguin.com*

Penguin Books Ltd, Registered Offices: Harmondsworth, Middlesex, England

A Monster of a Hamster first published in Puffin Books 1997

The Maths Wiz first published in the USA by Viking Penguin Inc. 1990 under the title *The Math Wiz* by Betsy Duffey with illustrations by Janet Wilson; first published in Great Britain by Viking 1992; published in Puffin Books 1993

The Roman Beanfeast first published by Hamish Hamilton Ltd 1996; published in Puffin Books 1997

This edition published by Viking 2000
1 3 5 7 9 10 8 6 4 2

A Monster of a Hamster text copyright © Elizabeth Hawkins, 1997
A Monster of a Hamster illustrations copyright © Mike Terry, 1997
The Maths Wiz text copyright © Betsy Duffey, 1990
The Maths Wiz illustrations copyright © Julie Anderson, 1992
The Roman Beanfeast text copyright © Gillian Cross, 1996
The Roman Beanfeast illustrations copyright © Linzi Henry, 1996
All rights reserved

The moral right of the authors and illustrators has been asserted

Printed and bound in Great Britain by The Bath Press

British Library Cataloguing in Publication Data
A CIP catalogue record for this book is available from the British Library

ISBN 0–670–89360–9

Contents

Elizabeth Hawkins

A Monster of a Hamster

Illustrated by Mike Terry

For James Barnes

Contents

1 *No School on Monday*

"QUIET, CHILDREN!" BELLOWED
Mr Pigott. "Now what do we have to
remember on Monday?"

The shouting that broke out from
Class 3 of Hopswood Junior School
shook the sprouting beans on the
science table and sent the terrified
hamster diving under the hay in his
cage.

Mr Pigott was new this term. How he
had got through his exams to be a
teacher was a mystery to Luke. The
dumbest teacher knew not to ask a
question of the whole class.

Mr Pigott waved his arms up and down like some bird that had forgotten how to fly.

"Luke Jones! Luke, ARE YOU LISTENING?"

"Who, me, Mr Pigott?"

"Come on, Luke. You tell me. Make it sharp now or the whole class will stay in after school."

Mr Pigott grinned happily.

The sudden silence was deafening. Every one knew it was the third episode of *The Monster's Revenge* on telly after school. The thought of missing it would have silenced an angel choir, let alone Class 3.

"The answer, Luke?" said Mr Pigott grimly, stroking his beard.

"What's the question, Mr Pigott? I mean, you can't expect me to hear with all this din. I mean, that's not fair, is it?"

In front of him Anna-Louise shook
her ginger curls over the back of her
chair and smiled sweetly, "Mr Pigott
asked: What do we have to remember
on Monday?"

"Anna-Louise. I am not talking to
you," boomed Mr Pigott.

"Monday, Pig," mumbled Luke, "I
mean Mr Pigott, it's a bank holiday. We
don't have to come to school."

"At last, Luke! I shall not have to look
at your miserable face on Monday. NO
ONE is to come to school."

"Yippee!" yelled one of the twins. He
was shushed and immediately pounced
on by the other twin and pushed under
the table.

The monster was going to break into
the castle for its revenge tonight and no
one intended to miss a single, spine-
chilling minute.

"One more thing," bellowed Mr Pigott

at the squirming children. "I don't suppose that a miracle could have taken place in this class of television zombies . . ."

Luke stared at Mr Pigott in agony. Mr Pigott was keeping them in to spoil their fun, Luke was sure of it.

"Would it be too much to hope that a kind, generous child would take the hamster home for the holiday? It will

only take ten minutes to give you the instructions."

The silence was as thick as treacle.

"I thought not. How could a class of TV-crazed hooligans care for a lonely creature . . .?"

Luke looked at his Superhero jungle watch. Seven minutes, thirty-two seconds to go till *The Monster's Revenge* started.

"I will, Mr Pigott," said Anna-Louise. "I'll look after him, then he won't be lonely will he? And Luke, you'll stay behind and help me carry the cage, won't you, Luke?"

2 Take That Rat Away!

ANNA-LOUISE HAD been born good like everyone else, at least so Luke reckoned, but unlike everyone else she had never learnt anything different.

Luke knew that because he had lived next door to Anna-Louise since they were both babies.

Anna-Louise never pinched people, or borrowed things without asking, or said unkind things about other children. This was odd enough, but oddest of all, despite all this goodness, Anna-Louise was always getting into trouble.

"Why did you have to ask for the

hamster?" puffed Luke, as he and
Anna-Louise struggled down the road
with the cage.

"I didn't ask for it," gasped Anna-
Louise. "Nobody wanted it. How would
you like to be unwanted and alone all
holiday in an empty classroom?"

"It wouldn't have noticed. Hamsters
sleep all day. Mr Pigott might have

taken him home himself, if you'd kept quiet. What's the time?"

It had taken more than ten minutes to hear what hamsters ate, how much water they liked and how the cage door must always be kept shut.

"I bet we've missed *The Monster's Revenge* . . . all for a sleeping hamster that couldn't care less."

"Oh Luke," wailed Anna-Louise. "It's all my fault. But it's not too late. We can catch the end of *The Monster's Revenge* at my house."

When Luke and Anna-Louise reached the shiny, green door of Anna-Louise's house they knocked hopefully.

At the sight of Luke and the hamster cage, the smile on Anna-Louise's mother's face bounced back like a rubber band. Luke might have guessed.

"What have you brought that rat

home for?" she shrieked. She pulled a neatly ironed, white handkerchief from her apron pocket and held it over her nose. "I will not have a rat in my clean kitchen," she snuffled.

Anna-Louise's kitchen was much cleaner than Luke's kitchen. It was the sort of kitchen you were only allowed to walk around in socks in case your shoes made the floor dirty. Anna-Louise had no little brothers and sister to mess it up and her mother was always cleaning it.

Anna-Louise's mother sniffed the cage.

"I knew it! It smells! A . . . a . . . tchoo! Take it away – a . . . a . . . tchoo! I'm allergic to rats."

The hamster woke up at the sneezing and rattled all over the cage with fright.

"What are we going to do with it?" said Luke glumly as Anna-Louise's

mother slammed the green door shut.

"I don't know," said Anna-Louise
sadly. "We could put it on the lawn."

"Your mother is sure to see it from the
living room windows. I bet she'd
murder it or something."

"She wouldn't, Luke!" said Anna-
Louise. "At least, I don't think so," she
added uncertainly.

"I know . . . why don't we put it
behind the dustbins," said Luke. "Your

mother doesn't like dustbins so she
won't hang about there looking for
anything."

So they squeezed the cage into the
gap between the dustbins and the
fence.

For the second time Anna-Louise and
Luke knocked at the shiny, green door.
It opened a crack.

"I hope you are well rid of that filthy

vermin," said Anna-Louise's mother.

Anna-Louise smiled her sweetest smile. "Luke helped me. Can he stay and watch *The Monster's Revenge* with me?"

"You're certainly not watching that rubbish. Besides it's *Gardener's Delight* on the other channel and I'm watching that."

What a miserable day, thought Luke, as the door closed behind Anna-Louise. First Mr Pigott, then Anna-Louise and finally her mother had ruined the treat he'd waited all week for. All the class would be talking about *The Monster's Revenge* after the holiday and he wouldn't have seen it.

Luke went home the quickest way. He climbed on to the dustbins, shinned over the fence and leapt down into his back garden. He could hear the hamster scrabbling in the cage from the other side of the fence.

"It's all your fault," he hissed through the hole he and Anna-Louise had made when they were little. "You're . . . you're a monster. That's what you are."

3 Escaped!

LUKE DIDN'T SEE Anna-Louise over
the weekend.

He and his family went to visit his
Grandpa and then on Monday they
went to the bank holiday fair on the
recreation field. Most of his friends
were there too, but not Anna-Louise.
Her mother thought fairs were too dirty
and crowded.

That night Luke arrived home late.

Would Anna-Louise's mother have
discovered the hamster? He'd better
check. Mr Pigott had said that he
would hold Luke and Anna-Louise

jointly responsible for the hamster. It could be difficult explaining away a murder.

Luke climbed over the back fence, landed on the dustbin and peered down into the dark. He reached down his hand and felt the cold bars of the cage. It was all quiet, except for the screech of the wobbly dustbin as he straightened up.

On Tuesday morning, Luke woke slowly.

"Luke, how many times do I have to call you?" shouted his father from the foot of the stairs.

On weekends and holidays Luke was the first up, but as soon as school started he got his old sleeping sickness back.

After breakfast Luke went round and knocked on Anna-Louise's green door. The door opened a crack.

"Is Anna-Louise ready?" he asked.

"She's taking that revolting rat back to school," came a muffled voice through the crack. "It will be the death of me if I so much as smell it."

The door slammed shut.

Luke found Anna-Louise behind the dustbins. She looked terrible.

"You look terrible, Anna-Louise! You're not going to cry, are you?"

"Look. It's gone," Anna-Louise groaned.

Luke looked in the cage, turned over the bedding and then shook the cage upside down. Anna-Louise was right – no hamster.

"But it couldn't possibly have escaped, Anna-Louise. Mr Pigott especially showed us how to latch the door shut."

Anna-Louise sniffed.

"I mean, hamsters can't chew through metal bars . . ." Luke's voice faded away. Visions of murder unfurled before him. "Your mother —" he whispered.

"No . . . no . . ." moaned Anna-Louise.

"But this is a cage, Anna-Louise, like

a prison cell. A hamster couldn't break out of it."

"That's just the point, Luke," whimpered Anna-Louise. "How would you like to be locked in a metal prison cell, stuck behind a dustbin, surrounded by smelly bags of rubbish, nothing to see, nowhere to play . . ."

Slowly the light dawned on Luke.

"You didn't . . . you didn't let it out, did you Anna-Louise?"

Anna-Louise nodded slowly.

"Everyone went to the fair yesterday. I had no one to play with and the hamster had no one to play with, so I thought . . ." Anna-Louise's voice trailed away.

Luke examined the dustbins. They were no longer on their concrete base. Someone had laid grass and twigs and leafy branches over the concrete. In the middle sat a silver pie plate from the

24

rubbish, filled with water, like a miniature lake.

"What's all this?" demanded Luke. Anna-Louise's mother would never allow such a mess.

"It's a safari park," whispered Anna-Louise. "It was for the hamster. I spent ages making it and he loved it, he really did."

"Did your mother allow it?"

"She doesn't know. She hasn't been out of the house since the hamster came. You should have seen the hamster, Luke. He ran along the branches, hid under the leaves, put his paws —"

"Did you put him back?" asked Luke sharply.

"Sort of. He loved it such a lot . . . I left the cage door open and built a fence of branches and leaves, so that he could have a run but not escape, but,"

Anna-Louise shuddered with a sob, "but someone moved the dustbin in the night."

Luke groaned. He remembered the wobble and the screech.

"What are we going to do, Luke? We'll have to tell Mr Pigott and he'll be cross enough, but my mother will be furious if she knows there's a hamster wandering the garden. She'll die."

Luke had heard Anna-Louise's mother say a lot of things would make her die. She never did.

It was all Anna-Louise's fault. Luke had a good mind to leave it to her to get them out of this mess.

But that wouldn't be any good. Anna-Louise had an imagination the size of a pea. She'd only go and tell and then they would both be in trouble.

"I know," said Luke. "We won't tell your mother or Mr Pigott. Somehow we'll have to think of a way of keeping them both off the scent, until we catch the hamster and get it back to school."

"What will we do with the cage?" said Anna-Louise tearfully.

"We'll stuff something in the hay and say the hamster is sleeping. Your mother will see us carrying away the cage with the hump in and think the hamster has gone."

"But what about Mr Pigott? He's bound to check to see if the hamster is all right."

Luke stared at the empty cage and thought.

"We'll keep him away – until we've had time to make a new one."

"Make a new what?" said Anna-Louise.

"In craft – the first lesson," said Luke excitedly. "We can use plasticine for the body, some yellow wool for fur and

those black beads for eyes . . . a home-made hamster."

"A home-made hamster! Oh Luke, you're a genius," said Anna-Louise, rubbing away a tear on her clean sleeve.

Sometimes, Luke decided, it wasn't all bad helping Anna-Louise.

4 A Pathetic Monster

"GOOD MORNING, ANNA-LOUISE and Luke," said Mr Pigott rubbing his hands together. "Refreshed from the holiday, are we? And good – the hamster is safely back I see. How's it been?"

"Well . . ." said Anna-Louise. "It's sort of . . . well . . ."

"Well, is it – just what I should hope to hear. Let's see how it has survived its little outing."

Anna-Louise almost dropped her end of the cage with fright.

"We'd better put it at the back of the

class, out of the sunlight, Mr Pigott,"
said Luke quickly. "It's asleep, Mr
Pigott. Sometimes holidays can be a bit
tiring."

"That's unusually thoughtful of you,
Luke," smiled Mr Pigott, flashing white
teeth in a scraggy beard. "I see you
have benefited from your holiday too."
The teeth reminded Luke of the
monster.

Luke and Anna-Louise set the cage at
the back of the classroom. Mr Pigott
was in a good mood. With any luck
Luke would be able to keep him away
from the cage.

"Luke," called out Mr Pigott. "Let us
continue your excellent start to the day.
Take the register to the headmistress's
office, and DON'T dawdle on the
way."

Horrors! Luke couldn't leave Anna-
Louise alone. Not only was she

incapable of keeping a secret, but she always ended up telling everyone.

"Ouch!"

"Come along now, Luke. Don't play the fool."

"Sorry, Mr Pigott," gasped Luke, doubled up over his knee. "Hurt my knee on the bumper cars at the fair. Mum says I've got to rest it."

Mr Pigott eyed him suspiciously.

"You were walking perfectly adequately when you carried the hamster's cage into the classroom."

"It was the strain of it, Mr Pigott. It hit me just when I put the cage down."

Mr Pigott stared coldly at Luke and drummed his fingers on the register.

"My mistake, Luke! I thought the little holiday had turned you into a responsible, caring boy. But," Mr Pigott's voice was working up like a steam engine, "you're the same unruly, wretch of a boy underneath. Right . . . who'll take the register?"

Anna-Louise's hand started to go up, but Luke snatched it down.

"As I have so many offers," bellowed Mr Pigott, "I will have to choose. Twins – you can't hide behind the door. You can take it."

Mr Pigott handed over the register to the twins.

Delia and David looked alike. They both had shiny, blond hair and baby big, blue eyes. With their big eyes and wide smiles they looked so innocent, that no grown-up would believe the terrible behaviour they were capable of.

Luke found an empty table in the corner for Anna-Louise and himself. He wasn't going to have anyone watching what they were up to.

"For craft this morning," began

Mr Pigott in a voice loud enough to fill a football pitch let alone Class 3, "I would like you to make that monster you were all rushing off to see on television before the holiday. In the boxes in front of you, you will find wood, scraps of materials, empty egg boxes and lavatory rolls, beads and buttons. The best will go on show for Parents' Evening."

There were shouts of "Wow!" and
"Fantastic!"

"But we missed *The Monster's Revenge*,"
moaned Anna-Louise to Luke. "I can't
remember what the monster looks like."

"Shut up!" hissed Luke. "We've got to
make the hamster."

"Luke, DO NOT TALK. Ah, twins –
you're back. Luke and Anna-Louise
have room on their table. I'm sure you

can set a better example to Anna-Louise than Luke."

"What are you making, Luke?" asked David, as his monster fell apart for the second time.

Anna-Louise opened her mouth, but saw Luke's scowl just in time. She went on carefully sticking bits of yellow wool to the plasticine body Luke had modelled.

Luke selected two shiny black beads and pushed them in for the eyes.

"That's a pathetic monster," said David. "It looks more like a mouse."

"I don't expect their mothers let them watch *The Monster's Revenge*," muttered Delia, as her toilet roll serpent rolled off the table for the seventh time. "Too frightening. I expect they watched *Gardener's Delight* or something."

"Shut up!" whispered Luke, as fiercely

as he dared. He was longing to ask if the monster got his revenge but he couldn't risk Mr Pigott coming over now.

"Right. Are you ready?" he whispered to Anna-Louise.

Anna-Louise went as pale as a ghost. To the twins' astonishment, she dropped to her knees and crawled along the floor. Luke followed carrying the plasticine hamster in his hand.

The twins' eyes opened as wide as full moons. This looked like something too good to miss, so they too dropped to the floor.

"Get off! We don't want you," whispered Luke hoarsely. "You'll get us caught."

Anna-Louise had reached the cage. With shaking hands she undid the latch.

"Luke's table – why do I have to keep

. . . what IS going on?" boomed Mr
Pigott.

Luke stuck his hand through the open
door of the cage and pushed the
hamster into the hay, until just its nose
and beady eyes stuck out.

The twins' eyes were the size of
saucers.

"Where are they? Where is Luke's
table? I'm not having this –"

Mr Pigott's voice was approaching
like machine-gun fire.

Delia's shining hair and blue eyes
appeared above the edge of the table.

"It's Luke's fault," whined Delia. "He
knocked my serpent off the table. We
can't find it anywhere."

"Here it is!" David shouted, as his
wide grin appeared above the table
beside Delia. In his hand he held
Delia's battered serpent.

"Well done, David," said Mr Pigott.

"Now get up all of you. And any more nonsense from you Luke, and you'll be spending the rest of the day outside the headmistress's office."

5 A Nasty Discovery

"WHAT HAPPENED IN *The Monster's Revenge?*" asked Luke eagerly, when he and David got out into the playground.

"I'm not going through all that," said David. "You should have watched it yourself. Why did you put your monster in the hamster's cage?"

"Even a hamster wouldn't be frightened of a pathetic mouse like that," added Delia.

"It's not a mouse," said Anna-Louise indignantly. "It's a hamster."

David and Delia laughed loudly.

"No, it's not. It's a cross between a

miniature, hairy mammoth and a
smelly, rubber ball," said Delia.

Luke saw that the whole thing was
getting out of hand. The twins
wouldn't be able to resist telling the
other children and then Mr Pigott

would hear. There wasn't much choice about it, he decided unhappily. He'd have to tell the twins and let them in on the secret.

"Promise not to tell."

"Course we won't."

"Cross your heart and hope to die."

The twins fell to the ground, dead.

"All right then."

Luke whispered the whole story hurriedly to them. "So if we can pretend to feed it without Mr Pigott going near it, we'll have longer to catch the real hamster."

"Amazing," said David.

"We'll help," said Delia.

The remainder of the day passed peacefully enough with Maths, P.E. and Story Writing. Class 3 were busy writing stories about the monster they had made.

Delia wrote about a serpent that only ate girls with red hair and she kept showing it to Anna-Louise.

David chewed his pencil and wrote one line: "Once upon a time, there was this monster", and got stuck there.

Luke wanted to write about the monster in *The Monster's Revenge*, but he didn't know what had happened. Instead he wrote about a monster that hid behind a green kitchen door and pounced out on passing girls and boys. The monster also happened to be afraid of rats.

Anna-Louise wrote a whole page in her best writing about a monster that looked like a miniature, hairy mammoth and smelt of rubber balls, but which was really a . . .

"You can't write that," said Luke, as he peered over her elbow. "Mr Pigott will guess. Tear it up."

"But it's the best story I've ever written," said Anna-Louise sadly.

"Go on, tear it up," ordered Delia.

The tearing sound ripped through the quiet classroom.

"What ARE you doing, Anna-Louise?" came a bellow from Mr Pigott.

"I'm tearing up my story, Mr Pigott."

"Did you say – TEARING IT UP?"

"It was a rotten story," said David helpfully.

"What a very SILLY thing to do, Anna-Louise. I hope it wasn't one of these silly, rude stories," said Mr Pigott smiling nastily. "But never mind. You can look forward to a pleasant evening tonight writing it all out again. At least four pages."

Mr Pigott stood up, looking much less cheerful than he had at the beginning of the day.

"Before EVERYONE packs up, whose turn is it to feed the hamster?"

Hands shot up on all sides. Luke pushed his way forward, waving his arm.

"Luke! Stop pushing! You and Anna-Louise had the hamster all through the holiday, but do you think of giving another child a turn? No, you don't. NO, LUKE. If I say NO, I mean NO. Now, what about Samantha? Ali? Ben? How shall I choose?"

The twins stood quietly at the back blinking their big, round eyes and smiling their widest smiles.

"Ah! David and Delia! Look at them, children. David and Delia have already, and without waiting to be asked, cleared their places and put their books away."

The class stared at them in surprise.

"So David and Delia it shall be."

If it was to be anyone it was best it was them, thought Luke with relief. Thank goodness he had let them in on the secret.

As the other children cleared their tables, David and Delia emptied the hamster's water bottle and filled it with fresh water. Then they filled up the nut and seed tray, and added fresh hay.

"It's all going to be all right, Anna-Louise," said Luke happily.

"Oh Luke, I don't usually like boys, but you're the best one I –"

Luke didn't hear the rest. A scream as good as any in *The Monster's Revenge* smothered Anna-Louise's words. It was followed by a loud sobbing from the back of the classroom.

"Delia, what is it?" called Mr Pigott. "David – are you all right?"

There was another scream and a few

more sobs as David struggled to speak.

"The hamster —" he sobbed.

"— It's dead!" wailed Delia.

Luke clasped his head in his hands. Why had he told them? Why had he ever thought he could trust them?

6 A Funeral

"DEATH," SAID MR Pigott, "is a most sad occasion."

A sob went up from Delia. It was catching. Samantha sniffed and Ali wiped his eyes on his football shirt.

"But animals, like humans, must die when they are old," went on Mr Pigott, delighted for once to have everyone listening. "It is part of life's natural cycle."

"What's he talking about?" said Anna-Louise with a worried frown.

"Old bicycles, I think," said Luke miserably.

52

The storm would break out any minute now, when the plasticine hamster was discovered. There was nothing he could do about it.

The children were pushing and shoving into the corner to see the dead hamster.

Ali poked his finger between the bars and into the hay.

"Ooh . . . it's cold and sort of sticky."

"It must have been dead a while if it's cold," said Delia.

"It's going rotten, that's why it's sticky," said David. "Dead things do, don't they Mr Pigott, like monsters?"

Luke couldn't wait to get Delia and David out in the playground. They would be cold and sticky by the time he'd finished with them.

"Thank you Delia and David," said Mr Pigott, "but that's quite enough. A sad end to our day, children, but it is

time to go home. I will ask the caretaker to dispose of the . . . er . . . corpse."

"Dispose of the corpse!" sobbed Samantha. "You can't throw out our lovely hamster like a bit of old rubbish. What about a funeral?"

"Yeah," yelled Ben. "Let's have a funeral."

"There's nothing good on telly tonight," added Ali helpfully.

Luke tried to shut his ears to the shouts going up on all sides in favour of staying late for a funeral.

Samantha volunteered to tell the waiting parents in the playground.

"It's not every day you get a death in the classroom," said Delia cheerfully.

Mr Pigott looked delighted with the children's enthusiasm. Never before had the children volunteered to stay late after school. Funeral announcements were designed on white paper with black pens. Floral wreaths were drawn on coloured paper.

"Luke," said Mr Pigott. "Not helping I see! You can take this note to the headmistress asking her to join us at the funeral. Let her see the quality of my class. And I don't want to hear a word about your knee. I saw you playing football in the lunch-break."

Mr Pigott straightened his tie and smoothed down his beard.

"Anna-Louise, don't look so shocked, dear. Believe me, I share your sorrow. Forget the monster story tonight and sit down now and write us a little poem about the hamster. You can read it over the grave."

Luke arrived back in time to see David and Delia dive into the hamster's cage with a spotted, pirate scarf from the drama box. They re-emerged with a neatly wrapped, spotted bundle.

Ali found an empty chalk box for a coffin. He decorated the sides with drawings of spaceships.

"So that its soul can travel out of this world in a spaceship. It's quicker than angels."

Soon the funeral party was ready.

Delia walked solemnly at the front carrying the spaceship coffin. Samantha sobbed behind her.

The children shuffled and jumped along, some giggling, some sniffing. Mr Pigott and the headmistress took up the rear with solemn expressions, broken only to stare sternly at Luke, who was trying to stamp on David's foot.

Last of all, the waiting parents followed the procession to the school garden.

"What a lovely, caring school," said a

mother, as she blew her nose hard with
her handkerchief.

David dug a hole among the
sunflowers. Delia and Samantha laid in
the coffin. Mr Pigott stood back and
waved Anna-Louise forward.

Anna-Louise took a deep breath and
read:

> "We had a hamster
> But he went away.
> Perhaps he'll come back
> One sunny day."

"Lovely," said Mr Pigott very loudly
so the headmistress could hear.
"Beautifully written. But Anna-Louise,
things don't come back when they're
dead, do they?"

7 *It's Not Over Yet*

"WHAT DID YOU do that for?" shouted
Luke to David, as Luke, Anna-Louise
and the twins set off down the road
home.

"It was brilliant!" said Delia.

"Fantastic!" said David.

"But you've ruined everything,"
groaned Luke.

"And I stuck on all those little pieces
of wool," said Anna-Louise sadly.

"Anna-Louise has a brain the size of a
pea," said Delia.

"And Luke hasn't got one at all," said
David. "Like a monster. Don't you see,

Luke – Mr Pigott would have discovered that plasticine, hairy mammoth. You'd have been in bad trouble. Now it's buried, he'll never know Anna-Louise lost the hamster."

"You should say thank you nicely to us for saving you both," said Delia. "Go on Anna-Louise, fall down and kiss my feet."

Anna-Louise looked down at Delia's dirty shoes and wrinkled up her nose.

"All right," said Delia, "you can give me three sweets instead."

Anna-Louise pulled a dusty toffee from her pocket.

"I've only got one."

"Oh no you don't!" said Luke, grabbing the toffee. "We'll need that to tempt the hamster."

"The hamster?"

"You never thought of that, did you?" said Luke fiercely to David and Delia.

"What's going to happen to the hamster running about in Anna-Louise's garden? What are we going to do about that?"

"You shouldn't keep animals in cages," sniffed David.

"That's just what I thought," said Anna-Louise. "I made this lovely safari park . . ."

"It's not a wild animal," said Luke. "It's a pet. How is it going to survive in the wild? It doesn't know how to find its own food or look after itself. It will be killed by the first prowling cat it meets."

"Oh!" said David.

Delia gazed down at her dirty shoes.

"We've got to catch it," said Anna-Louise. "My mum has an allergy to rats and mice and hamsters. She doesn't know the hamster is still in the garden. If she finds it she'll die and complain

to Mr Pigott and make him come and get it and then there'd be two hamsters and how would we explain that?"

"We won't have to explain," said Luke. "We'll catch it."

8 Still Searching

"I'M NOT HAVING all these children in
the house, Anna-Louise," said her
mother when she opened the shiny,
green door. "They'll make my kitchen
dirty."

"We're going to play in the garden,"
said Anna-Louise.

"Half an hour only. Then I want you
in for tea – alone."

The green door slammed shut.

Delia took a shoe lace out of her shoe
and tied Anna-Louise's toffee to it.

Luke searched in his back pocket for
the crumbs of the biscuit he had sat on

the day before. David found a cracked magnifying glass in his school bag.

"Where did the hamster go, then?" said Delia.

"I don't know," said Anna-Louise. She glanced nervously back at the living room windows. "We could look in the flower bed."

They dropped a few crumbs, swung the toffee among the flower stalks and

searched for tiny footprints with the magnifying glass.

"There are hundreds of tiny footprints here," said David. "What are hamster's footprints like?"

"They've got claws," said Luke. They would have to hurry. It wouldn't be long before Anna-Louise's mother checked on what they were up to. "Four claws and –"

Above them, a window sprang open.

"What are you doing in my flowers?" shouted the red face of Anna-Louise's mother. "Look – they're bent. They'll be ruined. Get off the flower bed – at once."

"It's too crowded in here," muttered Luke. "Let's lay a crumb trail on the lawn and tempt the hamster out."

The children scattered the biscuit crumbs across the lawn. No sooner had they got to the other side than the trail was spotted . . . but not by the hamster.

A cooing, a swooping, a flapping descended all around them.

"Look at that!" said David. "There are at least a hundred pigeons."

"A hundred – how do you know?" said Delia.

"I counted them."

"No you didn't."

The green door swung open.

"Get them off!" came a shriek Luke
knew all too well. "They'll mess up my
lawn."

Anna-Louise's mother emerged
banging a saucepan lid.

"Off . . . Off . . . Get off my lawn!"

"That's done it," groaned Luke. "The
hamster will have been frightened to
the other side of the moon by now."

"And as for you children," shouted Anna-Louise's mother. "You leave at once, do you hear. And Luke – I shall have a word to say to your mother. AAH! Look! My lettuces, my spinach."

Luke looked at the vegetable patch. Why was Anna-Louise's mother making such a racket? As far as he could see there wasn't much in the patch apart from a few empty stalks and a half-eaten leaf.

David and Delia were watching with interest. Anna-Louise's mother was crawling on her hands and knees over the bare vegetable patch, examining the stalks and making little screeching noises.

Anna-Louise trembled with fear.

Her mother reached the corner and examined the half-eaten spinach leaf. Then – atchoo! . . . atchoo! . . . atchoo!

Anna-Louise's mother leapt to her

feet, sped down the path, into the house and slammed the door.

"Can we come to your house again?" said Delia admiringly. "Your mother is much more interesting than ours."

"What's wrong with you two?" said David.

Luke was lying face down in the spinach leaves with Anna-Louise collapsed on top of him.

"It's all right, she's gone," said Delia. "You can get up now."

"I can't," said Luke. "It's the hamster . . . it's under my tummy."

9 Secret Plans

IT WAS DECIDED. They would put the hamster in the empty dustbin overnight. Anna-Louise lined it with the remains of her safari park and filled up the silver pie dish with fresh water.

"I'm getting in the council vermin exterminator tomorrow," Anna-Louise overhead her mother say, as she went to wash her hands for tea.

"There's a waiting list, dear," said Anna-Louise's father.

"I have a garden teeming with rats. That rat Anna-Louise brought home from school bred when it was here. I shall insist the exterminator comes at once."

"Yes, dear."

Meanwhile, over the fence, Luke's mother was finishing Luke's peanut-butter sandwiches for his next day's packed lunch.

"I can't find your lunch box, Luke."

"I'll put the sandwiches in."

"No. Give it to me, Luke. I'll wash it."

"I'll wash it."

"No. Give it to me," Luke's mother gasped. "What have you done to it? It's peppered with little holes."

"They're air holes."

"What do you need air holes for?"

"To air his sandwiches. That's obvious," said Luke's father putting his newspaper down. He gave Luke a wink. "Luke probably got attacked by bandits

with machine-guns on his way back
from school today."

"He's not getting a new one, that's for
sure," said Luke's mother.

However, David and Delia's mother
was delighted.

"Playing at Anna-Louise's house?
They've got such a lovely house and
garden. I'm glad you two are making
some nice, polite friends at last."

All three mothers were surprised when,
the next morning, Anna-Louise, Luke,
David and Delia woke on time and left
their homes early for swimming
practice.

Luke waited outside Anna-Louise's
house. She rushed out clutching her
swimming costume in front of her, as if
it might leap away at any minute.
Round the corner Luke popped the

wriggling swimming costume into his
lunch box.

David and Delia were waiting at the

crossing, leaping about with excitement. Luke wished David and Delia had never got involved. The way David and Delia were carrying on, someone was bound to wonder what they were up to.

"What's that sticking out of your school bag?" said Luke suspiciously.

"A spade, silly," said Delia.

"We're going to dig up the coffin," said David.

10 Breaking In

THE SCHOOL GATES were still locked.

"We'll have to climb over," said Delia.

"It's not allowed," said Anna-Louise anxiously.

But David already had his hands on the KEEP OUT – PRIVATE PROPERTY sign. He hauled himself up and reached the HOPSWOOD JUNIOR SCHOOL – HEADMISTRESS: MRS HARRINGTON; CARETAKER: MR TUMP sign.

With another heave David was over the top and had jumped down on to the other side. Delia followed.

"Here, hold the hamster," said Luke handing his lunch box to Anna-Louise.

Luke was over in a jiffy.

"Pass the box through the bars."

"It won't go," said Anna-Louise.

The bars of the gate were too narrow for the lunch box.

"You'll have to climb over with it."

"I'm not coming. I don't like heights. They make me all dizzy," said Anna-Louise miserably.

Luke, David and Delia stared at Anna-Louise through the bars of the gate.

"Take the hamster out and hand it through, stupid," hissed Delia, "and throw the box over afterwards."

Anna-Louise took the hamster out of the lunch box and passed it through the bars. Then she picked up Luke's lunch box and sent it crashing over the top of the gates.

80

Delia popped the hamster back in the box and started off across the playground with David.

"What about me?" wailed Anna-Louise.

"Leave her," called David. "We

haven't got time for sissies."

It serves her right, thought Luke, after all the trouble she had caused him.

"Go away . . ." Luke started, but he made the fatal mistake of looking into Anna-Louise's green eyes, brimming with tears.

"Come on Anna-Louise, you can get over," sighed Luke. "Don't look down. There you are . . . put your foot on MRS HARRINGTON. Now jump – I'll catch you."

As Luke lay squashed flat for the second time by Anna-Louise, he asked himself if any hamster could be worth this much agony.

David and Delia were waiting at the class garden. It was quiet. No one was around yet. The school looked quite spooky with no children and no teachers.

David, Delia and Anna-Louise

squatted down by the pile of freshly
turned earth. Luke picked up the spade
and began gingerly to dig.

"I bet it's turned into a real monster
in the night," said Delia. "A vampire
could have bitten it and changed it into
a vampire hamster."

Luke felt the spade knock against the
coffin.

"I've got the chalk box," he yelled.
"Look, here are Ali's spaceship
drawings."

"They didn't get too near space," said
David. "I reckon an angel would have
been faster."

Luke opened the lid. To his relief the
plasticine hamster was just as they had
left it.

"I think it's lovely," said Anna-Louise,
fingering the yellow wool she had stuck
on its back.

"Go on, you can have it to keep," said

Luke generously.

"Be careful, it might be a vampire," said Delia.

Luke took the hamster out of the lunch box and gently settled it in the chalk box. With care he punched breathing holes with a pencil in the lid. He was just laying the box on the path beside the garden, where every child would see it as they came into school,

when a roar went up behind them.

"Don't move. I've got you," shouted
Mr Tump, the caretaker. "I knew
someone had broken in. I've had phone
calls about vandals climbing over the
gate. You'll catch it!"

Delia and David squeezed in behind
the sunflowers. Luke hid the spade behind
him. Anna-Louise stood rooted to the
spot, her mouth a perfect, round O.

"I don't believe it!" huffed Mr Tump as he panted up. He stared, horrified, at the hamster's chalk box coffin. "What are children today coming to . . . grave robbers!"

11 Big Trouble

ANNA-LOUISE AND LUKE stood alone
in front of the class. Mr Pigott sat at
his desk with a stern, worried face. The
children waited with interest.

The door sprung open and in strode
Mrs Harrington, clutching a large, black
handbag like armour plating. Without
uttering a word she set the handbag
with a thump on the floor. Slowly her
chill, grey eyes swept the class, lingering
on Luke and Anna-Louise.

"Never," she began. "Never in all my
time at Hopswood Junior School have
we had such a distressing incident.

Digging up the resting place of your dear hamster . . . dear children, what could be a more terrible thing to do? Of course I blame it on too much television and unsuitable programmes. So I shall be sending a letter to all parents advising against any programmes with monsters, ghosts or the like."

A furious whisper broke out among the children.

"Quiet!" ordered Mrs Harrington.

Luke felt the grey eyes settle on him like a cloud, and shivered.

"As for Anna-Louise and Luke, words cannot express my horror. Fortunately you were found in time by Mr Tump, and also I might say by the twins – David and Delia, who had most thoughtfully arrived early to water the sunflowers. I shall of course call your parents and –"

The door swung open a second time and in hobbled Mr Tump, huffing and puffing.

"Look!" he gasped.

In his trembling hands lay the hamster, a real live hamster, busily nibbling a peanut-butter sandwich.

Words failed Mrs Harrington.

"I was going to bury the coffin again," huffed Mr Tump, "when I hears this scrabbling and snuffling. I don't mind telling you I didn't want to open it, but I sees this whisker poking through a hole in the box, and I opens it, and there I sees this creature eating this bit of bread . . ."

The class craned forward eagerly to watch.

Mr Tump snatched the bread from the hamster and sniffed it.

"Peanut-butter sandwich, it is."

All colour drained from Mr Pigott's

face as he stood up shakily and took the hamster.

"It looks like our hamster. Yes, it certainly does."

"It's a miracle, isn't it Mr Pigott?" called out Samantha.

"Probably just a ghost hamster," said Ali.

"It's sleeping sickness," said Delia. "I saw it on television. You think people are dead but they're not. They are in a deep sleep and if you're not careful they get buried . . ."

"Enough, Delia dear," said Mrs Harrington. "You really must not believe everything you see on these dreadful programmes. Now Mr Pigott, your class has wasted enough of my precious time. Next time, only call me for a funeral when you are quite sure there is a need for one."

Mrs Harrington picked up her black

handbag and marched out. Mr Pigott
blushed an angry red.

A happy chattering broke out in the
classroom.

"Be quiet!" bellowed Mr Pigott. "Yes,
Anna-Louise, what is it now?"

"You won't call my mother, will you Mr Pigott?" said Anna-Louise looking like a ghost herself. "Now we've got the hamster back . . ."

"Not this time," said Mr Pigott. "But any more of this nonsense and I will. Now who is going to put the hamster back in its cage?"

Children's arms shot up like a waving forest, except for the corner where Anna-Louise, Luke and the twins sat.

"It worked," grinned Delia.

"It was brilliant," said David.

"Tell me," said Luke. "What happened on *The Monster's Revenge*?"

"There's no point," said David. "You heard what Mrs Harrington said. We'll have to watch *Gardener's Delight* next week."

Luke groaned, "And I haven't even got any lunch. The hamster's eaten my peanut-butter sandwiches. I'll starve."

He would never, ever do anything for Anna-Louise again.

"You mustn't starve, Luke," said Anna-Louise anxiously. "You can have my lunch. I had a big breakfast."

"All of it?" said Delia, her eyes wide with amazement.

"All of it!" said Anna-Louise.

"No," smiled Luke. "We'll share."

BETSY DUFFEY

The Maths Wiz

ILLUSTRATED BY JULIE ANDERSON

For my mother

Contents

The PE Problem

Marty Malone was a Maths Wizard. He could add, subtract, multiply and divide better than any other first year junior at Danville School.

When he was only four years old he did his first subtraction problem. He was sitting on the floor with his baby brother, Tad. Baby Tad was sucking hard on his bottle. His chubby hands held the bottle tightly. His eyes were almost closed.

Even way back then Marty liked to think of everything as a maths problem. He watched the baby for a while. Then he thought:

BABY + BOTTLE = QUIET BABY

Then he started wondering:

BABY − BOTTLE = ??????????

What??

Marty always said that every problem needs an answer.

So he reached over and pulled the bottle away from Baby Tad. It wasn't easy. The bottle was right in Tad's mouth. Marty pulled with all his strength, harder, harder . . . *Pop!* The bottle popped out of the baby's mouth.

BABY − BOTTLE = ?????????????

For a few seconds there was no reaction. Then Baby Tad's eyes blinked open. His face began to wrinkle. It wrinkled more and more.

Then −

Waaaaaaaaaaaaaaaaaaaaa!!!!!!!!!

BABY − BOTTLE = WAAAAAAAAAAAA!!!

"What are you doing in there?" called his mother from the kitchen.

"Maths, Mum," Marty answered, "just maths."

Quickly he stuck the bottle back into the baby's mouth.

All was quiet again.

By the time he started infant school he already knew how to add and subtract, to carry and borrow numbers.

The summer after infant school he did his first multiplication problem.

He had only had his guinea pigs, Plus and Minus, for a month when it started. Plus had four babies.

Everyone was delighted.

His mum brought them fresh lettuce every day from the store. His dad brought home extra newspapers from the office to put in the bottom of the cages.

Tad, who was now no longer a baby, loved to hear them squeak. Every time the fridge door opened the guinea pigs thought it was dinner time and they would start squeaking. Tad was always opening the door just to hear them.

One month later, those baby guinea pigs were grown and THEY had babies! Then another month passed and THEIR babies were grown and had babies.

Marty was thrilled. He made a chart for his bedroom wall that looked like this:

$1 \times 4 = 4$

$2 \times 4 = 8$

$4 \times 4 = 16$

By the end of the summer he had thirty guinea pigs!

Everyone else was not thrilled.

His mother got tired of buying all that lettuce. Thirty guinea pigs eat a lot of lettuce.

His dad got tired of bringing home newspapers.

Everyone got tired of the *squeak, squeak, squeak*.

The multiplication problem stopped when Marty's mum called the pet shop to come and pick up all the guinea pigs. Only Minus got to stay.

Marty's mum made a new family rule:

THE PEOPLE IN THIS FAMILY MUST

ALWAYS OUTNUMBER THE PETS

She wrote it on a piece of paper and put it up on the fridge with a magnet.

At the bottom of the paper Marty wrote:

PEOPLE > PETS

Marty always thought that there was no problem too big or too long for him to solve.

He had a poster taped over his desk in

his bedroom. He made it himself with poster board and markers. It said:

MATHS WIZ AT WORK

NO PROBLEM TOO BIG

NO PROBLEM TOO LONG

But now Marty had a problem that seemed too big for him to solve. A problem that was making his life miserable.

He called it the PE Problem. He thought of it like this:

$$\text{MATHS WIZ} + \text{PE} = \text{MISERY}$$

Pick Me!!!

Marty had only been at Danville School for two weeks. Two weeks doesn't seem like a very long time if you are at the beach or on winter holidays, but the first two weeks at a new school can seem like a long, long time. It did to Marty.

It was long enough for Marty to find out two things that would cause his PE Problem. The first was that all first year juniors had to take sports lessons, called PE at Danville School. The second thing was that Marty Malone was the worst child in the class.

Being good at maths did not prepare you for everything in the world. Being good at maths did not prepare you for PE.

*

Marty sat at the desk in his bedroom. He closed the door so that Tad would not come in and bother him.

Tad loved to sneak into his room and break his pencils. He would take them one by one and press the point down hard on the table until, *crack*, the pencil would break. Then he would laugh.

Marty did not think it was at all funny.

He was supposed to be doing his homework but he kept thinking about his problem, the PE Problem.

What made PE such a problem?

He looked round his room. Anyone could look at this room and tell that Marty did not like sports. There were no golden football or basketball trophies on his shelves. There were no rounders pennants tacked up on his walls. No balls, bats or rackets were scattered across his floor.

So, Marty didn't like sports.

That had never been a problem at Marty's old school. He had liked gym class at his old school just fine. You didn't have to like sports or even be good at sports to have fun playing games with the other kids. Sports were fun at his old school.

Things were different at Danville School. Mr McMillian, the PE teacher at Danville School, had different ideas about sport. To him sports were not games for having fun, sports were serious business.

Worst of all was something that Mr McMillian called:

"CHOOSING TEAMS"

At the beginning of each class he picked two captains. He went down a list of the class alphabetically. Each day the next two on the list would be the Captains of the Day.

Everybody would line up on a black line on the gym floor, and the captains would take turns picking out the children they wanted to have on their teams.

First one captain would choose somebody, then the other captain would choose, until everyone was chosen.

Those who were good at sports were always chosen first. Those who had lots of friends were always chosen next.

Every day for two weeks Marty had been chosen last.

Being chosen last at PE was the worst thing about Danville School.

Marty put his head down on his desk. He remembered the PE lesson that morning. It still hurt his feelings to think about it.

As usual, the class began with "choosing teams".

Bob Cheatham was the captain of the red team. "I choose Tom Ballan!" he said importantly.

Big surprise, thought Marty. Tom Ballan was great at sports.

"I choose Tipper Grant," the blue team captain called out.

Tipper had lots of friends.

Marty's shoulders sagged. He looked down at a crack on the gym floor.

One by one the children were chosen. As their names were called they ran forward excitedly to the red or the blue team.

When they got to their team they clapped hands in a high five with the other players.

"All right!!!!" they yelled as they clapped.

As the children were chosen Marty tried to think about something else. He practised addition in his head.

$2+2 = 4 \ldots 4+4 = 8$.

It didn't work.

He could only think about the teams. A silent prayer kept calling in his head. *Pick me. Pick me.*

"Susie Bartow," the red captain called.

$8+8 = 16 \ldots$ *Pick me. Pick me*, his brain said.

"Randy Sims."

Pick me. Pick me.

"Julie Jackson."

Pick meeeeeeee!!!!

Slowly the picking went on and on. Still Marty stood on the line. Finally only two kids were left.

Marty looked up from the floor to sneak a peek at the other kid – Billy Beason.

Billy was in the highest maths group

with Marty. But in PE – well, in PE Billy
missed the ball when he batted at softball
and stumbled when he tried to run fast.

Billy was probably the second worst boy
in PE. Before Marty had started school two
weeks ago Billy had probably been the
WORST boy in PE.

Billy was looking down at his shoes, too.
He was used to being chosen last.

"Billy Beason," Bob called. He rolled his eyes up to the ceiling.

Billy began walking slowly towards the red team. The teams were already lining up at the volleyball net. Marty noticed that no one held up their hand for Billy to clap.

Being good at maths didn't get you far in PE, Marty had thought as he headed for the blue team.

*

Crack!

Uh-oh! Tad was at the pencils again. Marty jumped up from his desk and grabbed his pencil box. He pushed Tad out of the room. He had work to do. He closed the door and locked it this time.

He took out a blank sheet of notebook paper and put it on his desk.

The fresh white paper gave him hope.

He looked up at the sign over his desk.

He could figure this one out!

At the top of the paper he wrote:

THE PE PROBLEM

Then he wrote:

MATHS WIZ + PE = MISERY

He chewed on the eraser of his pencil for a minute as he looked at the paper. Then he wrote:

MATHS WIZ − PE = ???????

He had to get out of PE.
But how?
He drew a circle around the letters PE. Under it he wrote:

HOW TO GET OUT OF PE

He chewed on his eraser some more.
Suddenly he had a plan.
A plan that would get him out of PE.
In big black letters he wrote two words:

ACE BANDAGE

Then for the first time in two weeks he smiled.

The Ace Bandage Plan

Beep . . . Beep . . . Beep . . . Beep . . .

It was morning.

Marty reached over without getting out of bed and pushed the black button on top of his alarm clock. The beeping stopped.

He rested his head back on the pillow without opening his eyes. For a moment he imagined that he was back in his old bedroom before the move.

"Marty! . . . Marty!"

He imagined that he could hear his best friend from his old school, Jimmy, calling him to come outside and play.

"Marty! . . . Marty! Get up, Marty!"

It wasn't Jimmy. It was his mother! He pulled the covers over his head. She had ruined his daydream.

"Marty, get up for school!"

School!

Marty had almost forgotten his plan. He reached under his pillow and found the folded piece of notebook paper. He brought it out from under his pillow and sat up.

He held it tightly in his hand for a moment and then unfolded it.

He knew exactly what it said. But it gave him courage to see it again in writing.

HOW TO GET OUT OF PE
ACE BANDAGE

Marty got dressed in a hurry. He made his bed, brushed his teeth, and gathered up his homework and put it into his school bag. Then he made his move.

He ran into his parents' room and opened his father's sock drawer.

There it was, the Ace bandage.

His dad had sprained his ankle once on a hiking trip. Marty's mum had bought the Ace bandage for him at a chemist.

Marty remembered how he had put it on. The bandage was a long, brown, stretchy piece of cloth. His dad had wrapped it round and round his ankle – about twenty times. Then he had fastened it with two special clips to keep it from coming undone. It had been smooth and tight on his leg.

Marty poked the Ace bandage box into his school bag and headed downstairs.

Mission accomplished!

If he put the bandage on his leg then everyone would think that he had a sprained leg and he would not have to go to PE.

He could just imagine it:

Marty would come limping into the gym.

Everyone would drop their balls and rackets and come running over to him.

Slowly he would roll up the leg of his jeans and the Ace bandage would be wrapped tightly and smoothly around his leg.

"Ooooooooooooooooooooo!" they would say together.

The sports teacher would come hurrying over, filled with concern.

"Here, son," he would say, "lean on me. Come and sit down. No need for you to take PE today."

"It's nothing," Marty would say, waving them away.

"It's . . ."

"Marty!" his mum called again from the kitchen. "Come on down. You don't want to be late for school, do you?"

"No, Mum. I don't want to be late for school!" Marty answered as he ran down the stairs. And for once it was true.

Chubby Bubby Big Wad Chewing Gum

When Marty got to school he went straight to the boys' cloakroom. No one else was there. Everyone else was hurrying to class. The last bell was about to ring. He didn't have much time.

He took the bandage out of the box and unwound it. It was a lot longer than he had remembered.

He pulled up the leg of his jeans and tried to wind the bandage around his leg. It kept getting tangled. Finally he got it on.

It didn't look as smooth and tight as it had on his father's ankle. It looked bumpy and loose.

He looked in the box for the special clips. It was empty.

NO CLIPS!

He turned it over and shook it. He felt in every corner of the box. There were no clips in the box.

Marty didn't know quite what to do. He had got this far. He didn't want to give up now.

He checked his pocket – two five-pence pieces, one stone, one pencil stub, and one stick of Chubby Bubby Big Wad Chewing Gum.

He picked out the chewing gum.

Perfect!

He put the piece of chewing gum into his mouth and began to chew it. When it was nice and soft he stuck it on the end of the bandage. Then he stuck the end of the bandage down with the chewing gum.

Marty patted the bandage a few times to try to smooth it out.

He frowned. It did not feel very tight.

He stopped and thought for a second.

Maybe he should put the bandage back and forget the whole plan.

Brinnnnggg!

The last bell!

No time left to change his mind. The bandage would have to do.

Carefully, he pulled the leg of his jeans back down over the bandage and hurried on to the first lesson.

*

Marty stayed in his seat all morning. He was afraid if he moved his leg the bandage would come undone.

He could feel it slip a little every time he moved.

He didn't go to the water fountain. He didn't go to the boys' toilets at break time. He didn't even go to the pencil sharpener once.

Finally the bell rang for PE. Marty made his way down the hall. He tried to walk with his leg stiff.

Step . . . Thump . . . Step . . . Thump.

He kept looking down to check the bandage. It was already down round his foot like a sock. It didn't feel at all tight.

It was so loose that Marty could not feel it at all. It sure wouldn't convince Mr McMillian if it got any lower.

Step . . . Thump . . . Step . . . Thump.

He looked down the hall. He was almost

at the gym. Just a little farther.

Step . . . Thump. Almost there.

He glanced down to check the bandage again.

Marty stopped and stared down at his leg. He didn't want to believe what he saw.

There was a long brown tail coming out from the bottom of his jeans. On the end of the tail was the giant wad of Chubby Bubby Big Wad Chewing Gum!

What should he do?

Should he stop and try to pick up the bandage or try to make it to the gym? If he could get to the gym maybe he could fix it before anyone noticed.

He decided to keep on walking. He didn't have far to go. He hoped no one would step on the gum.

Step . . . Thump . . . Step . . . Thump.

He walked a little faster.

He looked down the hall to see how much farther he had to go.

Uh-oh! Down the hall, coming right towards him, was Mr Hardeman, the head teacher. Mr Hardeman was looking right at him.

He tried to make his face look as normal as possible. He tried to walk as normally as possible. He tried not to look like a boy with a long brown tail coming out of his jeans leg.

Mr Hardeman was a strict head teacher. He would not think it was very funny.

As Marty watched, Mr Hardeman came closer . . . closer . . . closer . . .

Mr Hardeman nodded as he passed Marty without looking down.

Whewwww!

He didn't notice the bandage!

Marty sighed with relief. All clear!

He stopped for a few seconds and leaned back against the wall of the hall to catch his breath.

He had made it past Mr Hardeman. Now he was almost at the gym door.

He stopped and looked down one more time to check his bandage.

At the bottom of his trouser leg he could see his bare ankle. He looked closer.

Double Uh-oh! No bandage!

He pulled up his trouser leg and looked one more time. He stared at his bare leg. The bandage was gone.

Marty felt sick. He decided that he'd better find the bandage and pick it up before someone stepped on the chewing gum.

He turned round and looked down the hall to find it.

No bandage.

Where did it go?

Marty saw something moving on the floor at the end of the hall.

Something long and brown.

Triple Uh-oh!

The long brown something was following along behind Mr Hardeman.

He could no longer see the Chubby Bubby Big Wad Chewing Gum. It was stuck to the bottom of Mr Hardeman's shoe!

Mr Hardeman must have stepped on the gum. The Ace bandage was still stuck to

the chewing gum, trailing behind the head teacher like a long tail.

He could see the other children in the hall turning to look at Mr Hardeman as he passed them. Some of them giggled.

Mr Hardeman nodded to each child as he passed.

Marty shook his head. Boy, would he be

mad later when he saw what had been following him. Boy, would he be mad at Marty if he found out who did it.

Marty felt even sicker.

He did not look back again.

Before he went into the gym he pulled his piece of notebook paper out of his pocket and drew a dark black line through the words:

ACE BANDAGE

Then he started into the gym for PE.

His plan had failed.

He was not going to get out of PE today.

Captains of the Day

Tweeeeeeeeeet!! Mr McMillian blew his whistle.

Marty stopped at the door to the gym. He still felt sick. His stomach hurt and his palms were cold and sweaty.

The other children pushed past him as if he were invisible.

He had seen a film once about an invisible man. In the film the man could do wonderful things because people could not see him. He surprised bank robbers at a hold-up. He listened in unseen on the plans of gangsters and stopped their crimes.

After the film Marty thought about how much fun it would be to be invisible. Now, after two weeks of feeling invisible at

Danville School he realized how wrong he
was.

He smoothed down his T-shirt and put
his hands in his pockets. He had worn his
favourite T-shirt today to give him
courage.

It was bright blue covered with white
numbers. The numbers made a long
problem. The problem started at the front
of the shirt: 2,345 + 4,563 − 3,678 + 9,561
− 2,890 . . . The numbers went on and on

all over the shirt. At the bottom of the back of the shirt was an = sign but no answer.

One night Marty had worked out the problem. It had taken him two hours to figure it out. 3,742 was the answer. Only a Maths Wiz could do a problem like that!

"Move *it*! Move *it*!" the sports teacher called out to the children.

The sports teacher used to be in the army. He still acted like a drill sergeant. He rocked back and forth on his heels and tried to suck in his stomach.

The children began to line up on the long black line that ran down the side of the basketball court.

PE was serious business.

Kate Ellen Johnson pushed Marty with her elbow as she passed by. Kate Ellen was always in a hurry. When she walked she moved her arms back and forth as if she were pushing people out of the way.

Sally Long followed her like a shadow.

"Sir, Sir . . . Sir," Kate Ellen called out in a high, squeaky voice.

"Sir, isn't it our turn to be Captains of the Day? See, we're up to the *J*s. Johnson should be next."

The sports teacher gave her a tired look and rocked back and forth on his heels some more.

Kate Ellen wrinkled her nose up as if she smelled something awful. She was always doing that. Marty hated it. It always made him feel like the something awful was him.

"See, we were up to Jenkins yesterday. Now we should be up to Johnson."

The sports teacher gave Kate Ellen a long, hard look.

"And then comes *L* for Long," said Sally like an echo.

"Move *it*, girls," he said loudly. "Line up now or there won't be any teams today – there will be LAPS to run."

Kate Ellen and Sally hurried towards the black line.

The sports teacher turned to face the other children. Some were not yet lined up.

"I SAID there will be LAPS to run," he said in a loud voice. "Would anyone like to run some LAPS today?"

At the sound of the word *laps* the class began to line up quickly. Nobody liked to run laps. Marty hurried over to his place on the line.

Why would anyone WANT to be Captain of the Day, Marty wondered. He could think of nothing worse than standing up in front of the class picking out the ones to be on his team.

He could just imagine it.

They would all be lined up on the black line.

The sports teacher would call out, "Captain of the Day, MARTY MALONE."

Marty would step forward from the black line and would call out his first choice.

"Tom Ballan," he would say.

"No, thanks!" Tom Ballan would say and he would head towards the other team.

"Tipper Grant," Marty would say.

"No, thanks!" Tipper would say and she would go to the other team, too.

Pretty soon the entire class would be on the other team.

It would be like one long subtraction problem. One by one each kid would be subtracted until there was only Marty left.

He would be left alone on the blue team.

Being Captain of the Day might even be worse than being chosen last.

If they were up to the *L*s, then the *M*s were next. Malone started with *M*. Tomorrow would be Marty's turn to be Captain of the Day.

He decided to be absent tomorrow.

Tweeeeeeet!

Uh-oh! PE was starting.

"Volleyball! Choose teams!" called the sports teacher.

Double Uh-oh! Marty hated volleyball.

"Captains of the Day . . . Kate Ellen Johnson and Sally Long."

Triple Uh-oh! thought Marty.

He settled in to be chosen last.

The teams were chosen. Last again!

Marty decided that today he would try as hard as he could. Today he would be good at PE.

The teams lined up and faced each other at the volleyball net. They took turns bouncing the ball back and forth over the net.

The sports teacher blew his whistle and the game began. Everyone was serious now. The ball went back and forth across the net and everybody tried hard not to miss it when it came to them.

Marty watched the ball closely. If it came to him he would be ready.

Finally the ball came high over the net right towards Marty. His big chance. His chance to get noticed.

"Get it, Marty!" someone called. They were cheering for him!

"Go, Marty!" He wouldn't let them down. This time he would hit the ball back over the net.

The ball seemed like it moved in slow motion as it made its way down.

Marty reached up his hands . . .

Kerthump!!

The ball hit Marty right on the top of his head.

Marty looked at his hands in disbelief. How could they have failed him?

The sports teacher groaned. The other team made a point.

Marty felt his face turn red. He moved to the back of the volleyball court. He was no longer interested in the game.

It was hopeless.

He kept his eyes on the floor and hoped that the ball would not come to him again.

When he looked up he could see Billy Beason on the other team staring at him.

He must think I'm a real wally, thought Marty.

He wished PE would be over. He looked up at the clock on the wall of the gym. In fifteen minutes he would be in Miss Williams's maths class.

Miss Williams was the one good thing about Danville School. Her class was wonderful.

It had problems, problems and more problems. And Marty was an expert at solving problems.

What was the solution to the PE Problem? Marty wondered.

$$\text{MATHS WIZ} + \text{PE} = \text{MISERY}$$

There had to be a way to make that problem come out differently.

Somehow, some way, today during the maths lesson he would solve the PE Problem.

But first he had to make it through PE.

Boy + Good at Maths = ????

Tweeeeeeeet!

"Take five!" yelled the sports teacher.

That was his way of saying, "Take a water break."

Some of the children went to the drinking fountain. Some of the others sat down on the benches and talked to each other.

Marty did not go with them. He was left alone.

At the other end of the gym Marty could see Tom Ballan. He stood out from the others, bouncing the volleyball on his knee. First one knee – then the other – then up to his head – then knee, elbow, head.

Wow. He was terrific.

If Marty was the worst person in PE, Tom Ballan was the best.

He was tall and was the only one in the class with muscles. He wore his T-shirt sleeves rolled up to the shoulders and was always stretching. Now he stretched out his arm and flexed it up. As he flexed his arm a real muscle bumped up.

Marty looked down at his own arm. He did not bend it up and flex it. He knew there would be no bump on his arm.

Boys with muscles were good at sports. Tom Ballan was always chosen first for volleyball and softball teams.

Marty thought of it like a maths problem.

BOY + MUSCLES = GOOD AT SPORTS

He thought of it another way:

BOY + GOOD AT SPORTS = ???

What?

FRIENDS, he decided.

BOY + GOOD AT SPORTS = FRIENDS

What was so special about sports anyway?

Why couldn't something HE was good at be considered special – like maths?

Marty sighed. He tried to make it into a problem:

BOY + GOOD AT MATHS = ????

He couldn't finish the problem.

He didn't think the answer was FRIENDS. But what was it??? He tried again.

BOY + GOOD AT MATHS = 'A'S ON REPORTS

'A's on reports sure were nice but right now he sure would like the answer to be *friends*, too.

If you can throw a ball or run fast, crowds of people cheer and go wild over you. You just didn't see crowds of people going wild over maths, did you?

But . . . what if they did????

He could just imagine it.

The gym would be filled with hundreds of cheering children. In front of a large blackboard would be Marty, his blue uniform shiny under the bright lights. Beside him in a red uniform, the challenger.

Tweeet! The teacher would blow his whistle and Marty and the challenger would begin to add long columns of numbers.

"Go, Marty!" someone would call out just like they had in the volleyball game. But this time would not be like the volleyball game. This time he could do it.

Everybody would cheer him on as he added the long columns of numbers.

"MATHS WIZ!!!!!"

"MATHS WIZ!!!!!"

"MATHS . . ."

Tweeeeeeeet!

The sports teacher's whistle interrupted his daydream.

"That's it for today! Move on out!"

PE was over.

Marty began to move towards the door with the other kids.

He had survived another day of PE.

"Move it! Move it!" the sports teacher called out, louder this time. "I SAID, move on out!"

"With pleasure!" Marty said softly to himself and he headed out of the gym door to maths class.

Triple Uh-Oh

The first year juniors were divided up for maths. Those who were the best at maths went to Miss Williams's room. The others went to different rooms.

Marty took a seat in the back row and began to organize his pencils. He had three pencils – all with sharp points. If one broke, he would always have a spare.

Miss Williams was passing out white sheets of paper. She placed the papers face down on the children's desks.

"We'll start the class with a time test," she announced. "Subtraction."

"Oh, no!" Marty heard someone whisper.

Marty smiled. He loved time tests. What could be more fun than a whole page of problems just waiting to be solved?

Miss Williams finished handing out the tests. She reached in her desk and pulled out a small silver stopwatch.

"You will have ten minutes." She held up the watch.

"Ready . . . BEGIN!" she called out as she pushed the button on the top of the stopwatch.

Quickly the children turned over their papers and began to work out the problems. If they finished all the problems before the ten minutes was over, they raised their hands.

Marty finished all his problems in only four minutes. His hand shot up.

Miss Williams hurried over to his desk.

"Very good, Marty," she whispered as she wrote *4 min. 20 sec.* on the bottom of his paper.

She smiled at him.

"You may work in your exercise book until the others finish."

Marty looked round the room. No one else was finished. Marty had five more minutes to wait before the test would be over.

He took out his exercise book. He opened it but he did not work in it. Instead he pulled his piece of notebook paper out

of his pocket, the PE Problem. He put it
inside his exercise book so it would look
like he was working in his exercise book.

He looked at the problem:

MATHS WIZ + PE = MISERY

He chewed on the eraser of his pencil for
a few seconds as he looked at the paper.
Then he wrote:

CHANGE THE PROBLEM!!

Last week in maths class they learned that if you change any part of a problem, the answer changes, too. In the PE Problem the answer was misery. Marty really wanted to change that answer. But what could he change in the problem?

He looked at the first part – MATHS WIZ. Maths Wiz was Marty. He was good in maths. He had tried as hard as he could to be good at volleyball. He just was not good in PE. He really couldn't change that.

He wrote beside MATHS WIZ: CAN'T CHANGE THIS and drew a line to where the problem said MATHS WIZ.

He looked at the next part – PE. Marty had already tried to get out of PE. All first year juniors had to take PE. He shook his head and wrote: CAN'T CHANGE THIS and drew a line to PE.

He chewed on his eraser some more.

*

"Marty . . . Marty Malone . . ."

Uh-oh! Back to maths class.

"Did you hear me, Marty?"

Double Uh-oh! Miss Williams did not
look happy.

"Uh, yes," said Marty.

"Then could you please give us the next
answer?"

"Answer??" Marty said. They were

checking the answers on the time test. He did not even know what problem they were on.

He looked down at his test paper, helplessly.

"Go ahead, Marty," Miss Williams said. "We're waiting."

Miss Williams did not sound pleased. She tapped her foot.

Tap . . . Tap . . . Tap . . .

Marty did not look up from his paper.

The class was silent. The only sound was the sound of Miss Williams's foot.

Tap . . . Tap . . . Tap . . .

"I know, Miss Williams!" a high, squeaky voice called out.

It was Kate Ellen, waving her hand wildly in the air. "I know, it's 68!"

"Kate Ellen!" Miss Williams said, turning to the other side of the room. "We do not answer out of turn!"

"Sorry," she said, sounding not one bit sorry.

Kate Ellen looked directly at Marty and wrinkled her nose and smiled.

She had saved him!

Marty began to like the way she wrinkled her nose.

He quickly shuffled his PE Problem under his test so that Miss Williams would not see it.

He looked down at his test and looked for the answer that was 68. Now he knew right where they were checking.

He hoped that Miss Williams would call on him again.

He raised his hand but she did not give him a second chance.

"Tom Ballan, could you give us the answer to the last problem?"

There was a long silence.

"234?" Tom answered.

"The correct answer is 334," Miss Williams said.

Someone giggled. Tom looked down at his paper and turned red.

Tom looked like he felt as bad as Marty had felt when he missed the volleyball in PE.

Miss Williams began to collect the papers.

"You may work in your exercise books

until the bell rings. Work the page numbers written on the board," she said as she walked down each row of desks picking up the test papers.

When she got to Marty's desk she reached down and picked up his test paper.

This time she did not smile.

Marty looked down at the spot where his test paper had been. The PE Problem had been under the test paper.

BOTH were gone.

Triple Uh-oh!

Miss Williams had the PE Problem!

A Note to Marty

Marty worked out a few problems in his exercise book. He tried to concentrate on his work but he couldn't.

He looked around the room.

Billy Beason was staring at him again.

He wondered why. He looked down to be sure his zipper was zipped. He licked his hand and smoothed down his cowlick.

Billy still stared.

He must think I'm a real wally, Marty thought again.

Marty looked up to the front of the room where Miss Williams was correcting the maths tests.

When she came to his she would know all about his PE Problem. Worse than that she would know about the Ace bandage.

By now he was sure that Mr Hardeman had found out about the Ace bandage on his shoe. He would be looking for the kid who did that to him. He would be looking for Marty.

Miss Williams would probably send him to the head teacher's office.

He tried to work out a few more problems.

Then he put his head down on his desk and closed his eyes.

"Psssst," someone hissed from the other side of the room.

"Pssssst!"

He looked up and saw a note being passed. He wondered who the note was for.

The class was good at note passing.

Kate Ellen had the note. She pretended to yawn. When she stretched out her arm she dropped the note on Susie Bartow's desk.

Susie tapped the back of Julie Jackson's neck with the note. Julie reached back and scratched her neck and took the note.

Julie put the note in her shoe and lifted her foot up high beside Bob Cheatham's desk.

Bob took the note and pulled a large rubber band out of his pocket. He put the rubber band around the note and pulled it back like a sling-shot. Then – *whooosh* – he shot the note directly on to Marty's desk.

Everyone giggled. Miss Williams looked up quickly from her desk.

"Class, is there a problem?" she asked.

"No, Miss Williams," someone answered.

"Then let's get on with our work," she said.

Marty waited a minute until Miss Williams looked back down at the papers on her desk. Then he looked at the note.

To: Marty was written on the front of the note.

Who could have sent him a note? he wondered.

He began to unfold the note.

Bbbrrrinnnnnggggg!!

The bell rang. School was over.

Miss Williams looked up from her desk.

Marty quickly stuck the note in his back pocket. He did not want to get into any MORE trouble with Miss Williams.

The note would have to wait.

3,742

The other children picked up their books and headed towards the door.

Miss Williams stood at the door and handed back the time tests as each one left.

Marty stayed in his seat. He couldn't decide. Should he wait until everyone left and then go up and get his papers from Miss Williams? Or should he try to slip on through with them?

He watched as each one got back their test. When they saw their grades some of them groaned. He watched Billy get his test back. Billy looked at his paper and smiled. Then Billy stopped just outside the door and looked back like he was waiting for someone.

Marty sighed. He wished that Billy was

waiting for HIM but he knew it wasn't possible. Billy thought he was a wally.

He decided not to go out until all the others were gone. He put his head down on his desk until he heard the last kid leave the room.

When he looked up Billy was gone.

Marty got up and moved slowly to the door.

Without saying a word, Miss Williams handed him his papers. He could tell by the way it felt that it was more than one

paper. He could tell that it was more than two papers. It felt like about three papers.

Marty moved like a zombie through the door and headed slowly towards home.

He was afraid to look at the papers. He carried them tightly in his fist, slightly crumpled.

He decided that one of the papers must be a note to his parents. He could just imagine what it said.

Dear Mr and Mrs Malone,

Your son has been in a little trouble today. He attached an Ace bandage to the head teacher's shoe with a wad of Chubby Bubby Big Wad Chewing Gum.

It was true. He looked down at the pavement. The pavement blurred.

His parents would have to sign the note and send it back.

They would not be happy about this.

Usually when Marty got home from school he ran right into the kitchen for a snack. But today he wasn't at all hungry. Today he went straight upstairs to his room.

He put the papers on his desk and smoothed them out. He sat down.

Then he took a deep breath and looked down at the top paper.

It was his time test.

$A+$ was written on the top line.

Miss Williams must not be too *mad*, thought Marty, *if she gave me an* $A+$. He began to feel a little better.

He moved the test paper to the side and stared down at the next page. It was the PE Problem, but something had been added to it.

Miss Williams had corrected it just like she corrected all his maths papers!

Under the problem she had written in red ink:

Another way to change the answer to a problem is to add something new to the problem.

Then she wrote:

MATHS WIZ + PE + A FRIEND = ??????

A friend?

A friend would make PE a lot better. Marty wished that adding a friend to his life was as easy as writing it down on a piece of notebook paper. It wasn't that easy!

He crumpled the paper into a ball and

threw it into his waste-paper basket. The PE Problem had caused him enough trouble.

That left one more sheet of paper from Miss Williams. It was not a note to his parents.

It was blue and was printed with big block letters.

Marty read it. Then he smiled.

MATHS CLUB PICNIC
WHEN: WEDNESDAY AFTER SCHOOL
WHERE: PLAYING FIELD
WHO: ALL MEMBERS AND
ALL STUDENTS WHO LIKE MATHS
WHAT TO BRING: PAPER AND PENCILS

At the bottom of the page in red ink Miss Williams had written:

The perfect place for a Maths Wiz
to find a friend!

Marty sat at his desk and thought about the maths club picnic. Lots of kids would be there – kids who liked maths like Marty.

He decided he would go.

Suddenly Marty felt hungry. As he headed downstairs to the kitchen for his snack, he remembered his note.

He sat down on the bottom step and took it out of his pocket. He quickly unfolded it.

It was the shortest note that Marty had ever seen. It had no words at all, only a number.

3,742

He stared at the note for a few seconds. Then he remembered –

His T-shirt!

3,742 was the answer to the problem on his T-shirt! He turned the paper over.

From: Billy, it said on the back.

Billy Beason! That's why Billy had been

staring at him all day. He was staring at the
problem on Marty's T-shirt.

Maybe Billy didn't think he was a wally.

Maybe Billy had been waiting for HIM
outside the door after maths class.

Marty wondered if Billy would be at the
maths club picnic.

Marty smiled again.

BOY + GOOD AT MATHS = FRIENDS

Maybe it could be true after all.

The Solution

The next day Marty ran all the way to school. Today he would solve the PE Problem!

He hurried down the hall to his classroom. Ahead he could see the door to Mr Hardeman's office. He walked a little slower.

He remembered the Ace bandage. He remembered Mr Hardeman walking down the hall with the Ace bandage attached to his shoe. He remembered the note to his parents that he had imagined yesterday.

Your son has been in a little trouble today . . .

Was he in trouble?

Was Mr Hardeman looking for him?

What had happened to the Ace bandage?

As Marty passed the door to the head teacher's office, he began to tiptoe. He didn't want to run into Mr Hardeman today.

Bang!

The door flew open.

Mr Hardeman!!!! Marty froze.

"Good morning, Marty," Mr Hardeman said. He nodded and hurried past Marty.

He didn't look at all mad!

He must not know!

Before the door could close again a hand reached out and put a waste-paper basket into the hall for the morning collection.

Marty looked down at the pile of rubbish in the waste-paper basket and smiled. Right on top was something long and brown and stretchy – the Ace bandage.

Mr Hardeman must not be looking for him if he was throwing away the evidence!

Marty started to pick up the Ace bandage, then he changed his mind. He gave it one farewell glance and headed down the hall to class.

He wouldn't be needing it any more.

The lesson began.

All morning Marty watched the clock.

The bell for PE rang and for the first time since he started Danville School the sound

of the PE bell did not make Marty feel sick.
He didn't mind going to PE.

He hurried to the gym.

Tweeeeettttttt!

Today the sound of the sports teacher's
whistle didn't bother Marty.

"Softball – choose teams," called the
sports teacher.

Today "choosing teams" didn't bother
Marty.

"Captains of the Day . . . Sam Miller and
Marty Malone."

Even being Captain of the Day didn't
bother Marty.

He hurried forward from the black line
to choose his team. He didn't feel at all
invisible.

He looked down the line at the kids in
his class: Kate Ellen, Tom, Billy, Sally and
all the others.

For the first time he saw them as

different people, not just as a group.

Some were good in PE, others good in art. Some were good in maths, others in writing. Every one of them was different. Every one of them was strong in some ways and not so strong in other ways just like Marty.

Today he was glad that he was good in maths. Maths was what he liked. Maths was what made him happy. So what if he was not good in PE? Everyone was not good at everything.

He stood tall and got ready to call out his first choice for the red team.

Tom Ballan and Tipper Grant leaned forward, ready to be called.

"I choose . . ." Marty said clearly and proudly . . .

"Billy Beason."

Billy looked up at Marty. His mouth dropped open in surprise. He had NEVER

been chosen first in PE.

His face broke into a big grin as he ran forward from the black line.

Smack!! went his hand against Marty's as they gave each other the high five. And together they broke into a yell –

"All right!!!!!!!"

MATHS WIZ + PE + A FRIEND =
ALL RIGHT!!!!!!!!

GILLIAN CROSS
The Roman Beanfeast

Illustrated by Linzi Henry

*To Jenny Cessford, whose class had the invasion,
and Liz Watts, who showed me the onagers. Thank you
for teaching my children about the Romans.*

Contents

1. Ask Molly

"YOU WANT TO win the *rhubarb pies?*"
Dad said. His voice came scratchily
down the phone from India. He
sounded very far away.

"Not the rhubarb pies!" Davey
shouted. "The *Roman prize*. We've all
got to make something for our Roman
project. We're going to choose the
winner when we have our Roman
feast at the end. What can I make?"

"*I* don't know," Dad said. "Why
don't you ask Molly next door?"

Davey sighed. That was what people
had always said, ever since he and

Molly started going to school. *Ask Molly.* Just because she never forgot anything, and she always knew what to say. Did they think he couldn't manage on his own? Did they think he *liked* being bossed around?

"But Molly wants to win the prize herself, Dad –"

The phone crackled. "Sorry . . ." Dad said, ". . . can't hear . . . ask Molly . . . Bye."

"Bye." Davey put the phone down and sighed again.

His mother came rattling down the stairs, with a wriggling twin under each arm and a blue bag of jumble on her wrist.

"Get down!" shrieked Luke.

"Down!" yelled Sarah.

"Not on your life," Mum said. She dropped the jumble, pushed Luke into one side of the double-buggy and

strapped him in with one hand. Then
she dumped Sarah beside Luke. "Did
you have a nice talk to Dad?"

Davey pulled a face. "I wanted to tell
him more about our trip to the Roman
fort, but the phone was too crackly."

"Never mind," Mum said. "He'll
phone again soon. When is the trip,
anyway?"

Davey's mouth fell open. Had she
forgotten? "It's –"

But before he could tell her, there

was a knock on the front door. Molly was standing primly on the doorstep, holding her pink lunch box.

"Have you got your packed lunch, Davey?" she said. "And your money for the trip?"

Davey's mum froze. "Trip?" she said.

"Didn't Davey tell you?" Molly's eyes widened. "We're going to the Roman fort today."

There was a loud yelp. "Davey! Why didn't you remind me? Where's the letter about it? With the form, to say you can go?"

"You put it in the airing cupboard to dry," Davey said. "After you washed Sarah's yoghurt off it."

Mum shrieked and raced upstairs. Sarah and Luke began to yell.

"Yog!"

"Want yog *now*!"

Molly shook her head. "Honestly,

Davey. You'd forget everything, if I didn't remind you."

"I *didn't* forget —"

Davey's mum came racing down again and fell over the blue bag of jumble at the bottom of the stairs. "Go on without us, Molly," she said, dashing into the kitchen.

"It's all right. I'll wait." Molly peered into the kitchen, watching Davey's mum cut thick slices of bread. "I've got salmon sandwiches and kiwi fruit. What's Davey having?"

There was no answer. Davey hoped Mum was putting *something* inside his sandwiches. She didn't always remember.

Two minutes later, Mum ran out of the kitchen, pushing the lunch into a blue plastic bag. She dumped the bag beside the buggy and snatched up her purse.

"Here's your form, Davey. And have I got five pounds? Yes – just!" She gave him the money and grabbed the blue bag from the bottom of the stairs. "Come on. Hurry!"

When they got to school, the coach was already there. Mum thrust the blue bag into Davey's hand.

"Have a good time."

"Don't worry," Molly said. "I'll look after him."

She pushed Davey into a front seat and slipped in beside him. Davey would rather have sat with Garry, or Jason, but he couldn't move without making a fuss, so he stared out of the window until they arrived at the fort.

When they got there, Mrs Johnson produced a bundle of quiz sheets. "Go round and find out the answers to these. Keep the partners you've been sitting with. And watch out for things to make for the Roman prize."

Molly jumped up. "Come on, Davey!" She bounced off the coach and ran towards the entrance of the fort.

Davey got stuck behind everyone else. By the time he climbed out of the coach, Molly was already at the main gate, scribbling the first answer on to the quiz sheet.

"We're supposed to be doing that together," Davey said.

"We are doing it together," Molly said. "You're just slow."

She ran through the gate, looking for the next answer and when Davey caught up, she was writing again. He looked over her shoulder, to read the

question, but she whisked the paper
away.

"Wait! I'll tell you the next thing
when I've written this."

They finished long before everyone
else. Molly tucked the clipboard under
her arm and grinned smugly.

"Let's go and spend our money."

"Money?" Davey said. "I gave my money to Mrs Johnson."

"That was your *trip* money, dummy." Molly pushed him towards the building labelled *Museum and Shop*. "Didn't you bring any extra money for souvenirs? My mum gave me two pounds."

Davey shook his head.

"Well, look round the museum then." Molly elbowed him through the door. "Try and find some good ideas for the Roman prize." She headed for the counter.

Davey was left standing beside a model of the fort as it used to be. He crouched down to look at it. There were tiny men playing games and cooking their dinner in cauldrons. And a wooden catapult, as big as a cannon, for throwing rocks at enemies in a battle.

Maybe he could make a model of that for the prize . . .

He studied the catapult until his leg began to go to sleep. Then he stood up and took a step backwards.

Right on to someone's foot.

"Sorry," he muttered.

There was a loud giggle from the counter. "You are a *dummy*!" Molly said. "Who d'you think you're talking to?"

Davey turned round. The person behind him wasn't a person at all. It was a life-size model of a tall Roman soldier with a funny little mouth and bushy eyebrows. And a very big red nose.

"Julius Sneezer!" Davey said, before he could stop himself.

Molly giggled again. "You dummy. You're talking to a *model*!"

"I'm *not*!"

It was too late. "Hey, everyone!"
Molly shouted. "Look at Davey's new
friend! He's found another dummy!"

There was an explosion of sniggers.
Whirling round, Davey saw the rest of
the class standing in the doorway.
Laughing at him.

Mrs Johnson clapped her hands. "I don't know what's so funny, but you can stop giggling. It's time to fetch your packed lunches from the coach."

"Come on," said Molly. She dragged Davey to the coach and picked up his blue bag. "It doesn't feel as if *you've* got much."

It didn't look like much, either. Davey took the bag and opened it. It wasn't much. Mum had picked up the wrong bag. *She'd left his lunch and given him the jumble!*

He tried to hide it, but Molly's hand dived into the bag.

"Look, everyone! Look what Davey's got for lunch!"

And she pulled out a huge brown T-shirt with a hole in.

2. *The Onager*

NEXT TIME DAD phoned it was from Singapore. "How was the Roman fort?"

Davey wasn't going to tell anyone about the T-shirt. Mum knew about his lunch being left at home, but not about the jumble bag. He'd hidden it right at the back of his wardrobe.

"Well?" said Dad. "Did you see anything to make for the rhubarb pies?"

"There was a machine for throwing rocks."

"A machine for *sewing socks*?"

"Not socks," Davey said. *"Rocks!* Like a giant catapult."

"I know," said Dad. "An onager. That would be a good thing to make. Can you manage it before that feast of yours?"

Davey frowned. "If I can remember it well enough. Have we got a picture of one?"

"I don't think so. Maybe Molly has. She's got lots of books."

"I don't want to ask Molly —"

But the phone went funny. Suddenly Dad wasn't there any more. Davey put the receiver down and went into the kitchen. Luke and Sarah were having their tea, and Mum had spaghetti hoops on her jumper and grated cheese in her hair.

"Have we got any wood?" Davey said.

Mum frowned. "I don't think so. Perhaps Molly has."

"I don't want to ask Molly —"

Too late. Just at that moment, Molly walked past, on her way back from the shop. Davey's mum pushed the window open.

"Molly dear, have you got any wood? Davey needs some to make a — to make a *what*, Davey?"

Davey hung his head. "One of those catapults at the Roman fort," he muttered.

"Oh!" said Molly. "You mean an *onager*." She looked hard at Davey. "Is it for the Roman prize?"

"Maybe," Davey said carefully.

Molly gave a bright smile. "I've got lots of wood. Come round!"

She took Davey into the shed and found some bits of wood and a handful of nails. And she showed him the picture of the onager in her encyclopaedia.

But only for one minute. Then she snapped the book shut and tucked it under her arm. "That's enough," she said. "I've got something important to do now."

She pushed Davey out and slammed the door after him. As he went home, he heard her go back into the shed and start hammering. *That's funny*, he thought. *What can she be making?* But he

didn't have time to worry about it. He
went into his garage and began to sort
out the wood she'd given him.

None of it was quite the right shape.
And he couldn't remember the picture
properly, because he hadn't seen it for
long enough. But maybe he could
make a sort of onager, almost as big
as a real one, if he nailed that long bit

of wood *there*. And the little bit across the top . . .

He worked for two hours. When his mother came to find him, he was just fixing the last piece of wood.

"Wow!" said Mum. "Is that it?"

Davey nodded. "Can I take it to school tomorrow?"

"Take it to *school*?" Mum gulped. "I suppose so. We'll balance it on the buggy, and Luke and Sarah can take turns to walk."

It wasn't easy. Mum had to push the buggy with one hand and hold on to a twin with the other. And Davey had to walk bent double, to stop the onager falling out of the buggy seat.

Luke and Sarah thought it was wonderful.

"Dayday!" gurgled Luke, who was in the buggy. Opening his mouth, he took out a piece of toast, left over

from breakfast, and squashed it into Davey's ear.

"*My* Dayee!" screeched Sarah. She tottered over and pulled Davey's hair. He wouldn't have minded, but her hands were covered in porridge. By the time they got to school, he needed a bath.

He heaved the onager off the buggy. "Thanks, Mum."

"Are you sure you can manage?" his mother said anxiously.

"I'll be fine," Davey said. Why did she always treat him as if he was two? "Bye, Mum."

He staggered off, with the onager in his arms. It was so big he couldn't see round it. By the time he reached the door, he had bumped into five people and three trees, and his arms were aching. But he managed to stumble down the corridor to his classroom.

As he tottered in, he heard Mrs Johnson gasp.

"What a wonderful onager!"

Davey grinned and put it down. "Thank you."

Then he realized that she wasn't talking to him at all. She was looking at another wooden model, on the other side of the room. It was twice the size of his, and it looked *exactly* like the onager in Molly's encyclopaedia.

Molly was standing beside it, with a grin all over her face.

"It's nothing." She caught sight of Davey and grinned even harder. "Hallo, dummy! You've got porridge in your hair."

Davey scowled at her. Then he looked at Mrs Johnson. "*I* made an onager too."

"So you did!" Mrs Johnson said

216

brightly. "Very nice, dear. Maybe next time you'll have an idea of your own."

"It *was* my idea," Davey muttered.

But no one noticed, because Molly came sailing across the room. She grabbed the rock-throwing arm of Davey's model. "Does this onager work?"

"Let go!" said Davey. "It doesn't —"

But Molly ignored him. With a heave, she tugged the arm backwards. It snapped off at the bottom, and she was left holding a long piece of wood, with a little piece nailed across the top.

"Oh dear!" she said pathetically. As if she wanted to cry.

Mrs Johnson patted her shoulder. "Never mind, dear. Accidents will happen. Davey can take it home and mend it, can't you, Davey?"

Davey nodded, crossly. But he knew he couldn't take the whole onager, because Molly's mum was fetching him, and she wouldn't have a buggy. All he could carry was the broken piece of wood.

He took that home, hoping there would be something to fix on the bottom, so that he could join it all up

at school next day. But he couldn't
find anything.

He ended up hiding the wood in his
wardrobe, right at the back. Next to
the bag with the brown T-shirt.

He would have to think of
something else to make.

3. The Fly Blind

"YOU COULD MAKE a fly blind," Dad
said.

At least, that was what Davey heard.
The phone was even more crackly this
time. Dad was phoning from Fiji.

"Who wants a blind fly?" Davey
said.

"I said a *fly blind*!" Dad shouted.
"*You* know! A strip of paper with us at
one end and the Romans at the other.
And ten centimetres for every hundred
years in between."

Suddenly it all made sense. "Oh,"
said Davey. "You mean a *time-line*!"

"That's what I said." His father's voice faded for a moment. When it came back, he was saying, " . . . you could look up lots of dates in the library."

"Oh yes!" Davey grinned. "I could do the Second World War, and the Vikings, and the first car, and –"

"And Henry the Eighth, and the Battle of Hastings, and –"

Glug! The phone went dead. Davey waited, but Dad didn't come back, so he put the receiver down and raced up to the bathroom.

"Mum! I want to go to the library!"

Mum was washing Weetabix off Luke's ears. "We-ell –"

"Libey!" Sarah's eyes lit up. "Me *like* libey!"

"Books!" said Luke. He hit Sarah with the flannel.

Mum pulled a face. "We'll go after

school. But we can't stay long. You know what the twins are like."

"I'll be like lightning!" Davey said.

But lightning wasn't fast enough. The moment they arrived at the library, Luke and Sarah raced across to the picture book box. They began to pull out all the books and hurl them on the floor.

Davey grabbed an encyclopaedia

and began to scribble down dates. *William the Conqueror – 1066 . . . Second World War – 1939-1945 . . . First man on the moon – 1968.*

While Mum put the picture books back, the twins charged off in opposite directions, heading for the shelves. The librarian chased Luke, and Mum ran after Sarah.

And Davey leafed frantically through the encyclopaedia. *Guy Fawkes – 1605 . . . first postage stamp – 1840.*

"We'll have to go!" Mum called. She tucked Sarah under one arm as the librarian cornered Luke.

"One more minute," Davey said. "Please!"

"No – now!" Mum said. "Or something terrible will happen."

It did. Luke dived at a book spinner and sent it crashing to the floor. Books showered everywhere.

"Oh dear!" said a voice from the
library door. "Luke and Sarah *are*
being naughty, aren't they?"

It was Molly, with her father.

Davey's mother waved to them as
she grabbed Luke. "Come on, Davey.
We're going *now*. You'll have to make
your time-line with what you've got."

Molly's eyes gleamed. "Is Davey
making a time-line?"

Davey saw her peering at his bits of

paper as he scooped them off the
table and hurried after Mum.

He spent the whole evening working
on the time-line. He cut out a thin
strip of brown wrapping paper, three
metres long, and measured it into ten
centimetre lengths. Then he wrote
down all the dates he'd looked up, in
the right places on the line. There
were almost enough.

As he coiled it up, Mum came down

from bathing the twins. She smiled. "Mrs Johnson's going to be really pleased."

"Mmm." But Davey had a nasty feeling that she wasn't going to be pleased with *him*.

Molly came round next morning with a huge coil of paper, as big as a cartwheel.

"Mrs Johnson is going to love this!" she said.

Davey didn't say anything, but he pushed his time-line into his pocket before Molly noticed it.

Mrs Johnson went quite pale when she saw what Molly had brought. "It's huge! What is it?"

"It's a time-line," Molly said proudly. "It goes back two thousand years! Look!"

"There may not be enough room –" Mrs Johnson began.

226

But Molly was already undoing the end of the roll. NOW, it said, in big black letters. She pushed it into Davey's hands.

"Hold this while I unroll the rest."

"Wait —" Mrs Johnson said.

But Molly didn't wait. She began to walk backwards, slowly unrolling the paper. As she went, Davey could see

things written on it. *Birth of Molly
James . . . Birth of Mrs James . . . Birth of
Mr James . . . Birth of Grandma James . . .*

By that time, Molly had reached the
window, but she wasn't put off. "Hold
this, Garry," she said. "I'm going
outside."

Before Mrs Johnson could stop her,
she ran out of the classroom and
appeared on the other side of the
window, tapping on the glass. Garry

undid the catch and she took the roll of paper and began to move backwards across the playground. Back and back and back . . .

For the first few metres, Davey could still read things on the paper. *Queen Victoria dies . . . the Great Exhibition . . . the Railway Age . . .* Then Molly got too far away.

When she was half across the playground, the other children began slipping outside, to cheer her on. Mrs Johnson had to go out too, to keep them quiet, and Davey was left on his own.

Stuck.

He was still holding his end of the paper – the end that said NOW – while the other children walked further and further back into the past. He couldn't go and join them. And he couldn't let go of the paper, or it would disappear through the window.

Every now and then, as Molly unwound the roll, there was a little tug. To stop the strip snapping, Davey had to take a step forward. Gradually, he was pulled nearer and nearer the window. He watched anxiously, to see how much further Molly would go.

He was so busy watching Molly that he didn't watch his feet. When he stepped forward again, he put his foot in the waste paper basket and lost his balance. He crashed to the ground, jerking the whole time-line.

Over on the other side of the playground, there was a R-RIP! With a rustle, the paper came curling back through the window, cascading on to Davey's head. Molly roared, and came thundering back across the playground.

"YOU DUMMY! YOU'VE RUINED MY TIME-LINE!"

"That was very careless, Davey,"
said Mrs Johnson, from behind her.
"You ought to make a time-line
yourself. Then you'd see how much
work it takes."

"I –" Davey put a hand into his
pocket and touched the tight little coil
of his own time-line. But he didn't
take it out and show it to Mrs
Johnson. It felt small and silly.

When he got home, he threw it into
his wardrobe.

4. Top Secret!

DAVEY DIDN'T RISK telling anyone about his next idea. Not even Dad, when he phoned from Australia.

"It's a secret."

"A *sea trip*?" said Dad.

"No! A – oh, never mind. I'll tell you when I've finished."

Davey put the phone down and counted his pocket money carefully. He knew just what he was going to do. On Saturday he went into town with Mum and bought three things.

A giant balloon.

A packet of wallpaper paste.

A tin of silver paint.

When he got home, he took a pile of old newspapers up to his bedroom. Then he blew up the balloon and tied a knot in it.

The bedroom door flew open.

"Loon!" said Sarah. "Want loon!"

Davey frowned at her. "Go away."

He put the balloon on top of the wardrobe and went into the bathroom, to mix the wallpaper paste. When he came back, Luke had arrived. He and Sarah were trying to shake the wardrobe, to make the balloon fall down.

Davey pushed them out and shut the door. Then he pulled his armchair across, to stop them getting back in. He needed peace and quiet. He'd made things out of papier mâché before, but only at school.

Slowly and carefully, he tore the

newspaper into strips. He pasted the strips all over the balloon – except at the end, where the knot was. When the layer of paper was thick enough, he put the balloon back on top of the wardrobe.

"What's that?" said Mum, when she came in at bedtime.

"A secret," Davey said.

He didn't tell anyone, even though the papier mâché took a week to dry. And when Molly came round, they stayed in the garden, playing on the climbing frame. Davey wasn't taking any chances.

After a week, the papier mâché was hard. Davey lifted it down from the wardrobe and stuck a pin into the balloon. It collapsed, leaving a shape like a ball with the end chopped off. He put it back on the wardrobe and he went downstairs.

"Have you got an old eggbox, Mum? I need three of those little bobbles that the eggs go in. And a piece of wire."

His mother looked at him. "For your secret?"

"*Maybe*," Davey said carefully.

He glued the eggbox bobbles on to the bottom of the papier mâché, to make three little feet, and bent the

wire into a handle across the opening.
Then he stepped back to look.

It was brilliant. Just like the
cauldrons in the model fort – except
that it was big enough to cook a *real*
soldier's dinner. The only thing wrong
was the colour, and he was going to
change that.

He opened his wardrobe and took
out the tin of silver paint.

By Monday morning, the cauldron
was finished – and it was still a secret.
Davey took it downstairs in a carrier
bag.

Mum grinned. "Do I get a peep?"

Davey almost showed her. Then he
thought, *Suppose she says something when
Molly comes?*

"You can see it tomorrow," he said.

When Molly knocked on the door,
he was standing in the hall with his

coat on, and the bag clutched firmly
in both hands.

"What's *that*?" Molly said.

"You'll see," said Davey. "When I
show Mrs Johnson."

All the way to school, Molly nagged
him to let her see. She promised him a
piece of chewing gum. She said she
would do all his sums. She even
offered to lend him her encyclopaedia.
But Davey didn't give in. He held the
bag tightly shut, thinking of the
beautiful silver cauldron inside.

He and Molly went into the

cloakroom, side by side, and took off their coats.

"Just a tiny, weeny *peep*?" Molly said.

"No." Davey put the bag on the floor, behind him, and kept his eye on Molly. Ready to grab the bag if she turned round to look in.

But she didn't turn round. What she

did was much worse. When she had
hung up her coat, she took one long,
fast step backwards. Davey didn't have
a chance to move before her foot
came down – CRUNCH! – right on
top of the bag.

"Oh *dear*!" she said.

Davey bent down and pulled out the
cauldron. It was ruined. Molly's foot
had crashed on to it, squashing the
front. No one could possibly have
cooked anything in a cauldron like
that.

Molly peeped over his shoulder. "I
could help you mend it. If you tell me
what it is."

Davey shook his head. Picking
up the bag, he ran out into the
playground. His mother was standing
by the gate, talking. He pushed the
carrier bag into her hand.

"Please – take it home again."

His mother looked at him. Then she
looked at the bag. "Are you going to
show me?"

"Show!" gurgled Luke.

"See! See!" shouted Sarah.

All the other grown-ups turned
round and Davey backed away,
shaking his head. "No. Don't look.
Just – put it in my wardrobe."

He walked slowly back into school.
What was he going to do now?

5. Invasion!

"I CAN'T COME to school yet," Davey
said on Tuesday. "Dad said he might
phone."

Molly grabbed his arm. "We'll be
late for school, dummy."

"I don't care," Davey said, tugging
the arm free.

Molly stamped off down the path in
a bad temper. She wasn't used to
Davey arguing with her. But Dad
didn't phone.

At ten to nine, Mum looked up at
the kitchen clock. "Look at the *time*!
Where's Molly?"

"She came," Davey said. "But I sent her away."

"Why didn't you *tell* me?" shrieked Mum. "Now you're late!"

She threw Luke and Sarah into the buggy, without even taking their bibs off, and made Davey run all the way to school.

"The play – ground will be – empty," panted Mum. "Every – body – will be – inside."

Davey thought so too, but he was wrong. All the other classes had gone in, but Mrs Johnson's class was still outside. Davey stared. Why were they having extra playtime?

He soon found out, when Mrs Johnson sent them in. Their classroom was full. All the children from Mr Morris's class had come in, and they were sitting in *their* chairs. With *their* things.

Molly took one look, and yelled.

"Keep your hands off my work, Sally Jones!"

Sally just laughed. Molly ran across and tried to shake her out of the chair, but it was no use. Sally held on tightly and laughed even more.

People began to get angry. They grabbed their folders. They pushed at the people in the chairs. They shouted. For a moment it looked as if there was going to be a real fight.

Then the bell rang.

Not the electric bell for break, but the big brass bell from Mrs Johnson's shelf. She stood in the doorway and swung it until everyone was quiet.

"Thank you very much, Mr Morris's children," she said. "An excellent invasion. You can go back to your own room now."

Grinning, Mr Morris's class stood up and squeezed out of the room. Molly seized her chair and sat down firmly.

"That was *horrible*!"

Mrs Johnson smiled. "Didn't you like it?"

"No!" Molly said. "I wanted to thump them!"

Mrs Johnson picked up a pen and wrote on the board – *wanted to thump*

them. "How did the rest of you feel
about being invaded?"

"Furious!" said Amy.

Mrs Johnson wrote *furious*
underneath *wanted to thump them.*
"What else?"

Suddenly everyone got the idea.
Words began flooding out of their
mouths; . . . *angry* . . . *they were stealing*
. . . *frightened me* . . . Mrs Johnson wrote
everything on the board. Then she
stood back, and put the pen down.

"Maybe the Ancient Britons felt like
you, when they were invaded by the
Romans. Pretend you're Ancient
Britons, and write a story about the
Romans marching into your village."

Molly stopped scowling. "Great!"
She took some paper and began to
scribble. Davey read the words over
her shoulder.

The Romans are wicked and cruel. They

came to our village and burned down all the houses. I had to save everyone.

Was it really like that, Davey wondered? Were all the Romans horrible and ferocious? Or were some of them like that Roman soldier in the museum? Julius Sneezer.

Remembering Julius Sneezer made him grin. He began to write.

We were all in the hut when this Roman soldier barged in. He was a real dummy. He fell over his own sword and his helmet fell off into our corldron. He wasent very braive . . .

Molly leaned over. "That's silly. And you don't spell brave like that." She stretched across and scribbled out the *i*. "You've got cauldron wrong too."

Davey stopped grinning. He made some sentences, using the words on the board. *I was furious. I wanted to thump him.* Then he got stuck.

"Oh Davey," Mrs Johnson said. "Can't you do better than that? Look at Molly. She's written three pages."

"I'm going to take it home and do lots more." Molly smirked at Davey. "I'll come round and read it to you."

She did. She came after tea, when Davey was sitting by the phone, playing shops with Luke and Sarah.

They had packets of things from the kitchen spread out on a box. Molly pushed everything on to the floor, and sat on the box.

"Ready?" she said. "It's really good. She started to read. *"The Romans are wicked and cruel . . ."*

Davey started picking up packets from the floor, but he wasn't quick enough. Sarah got hold of the soap.

She pulled off the paper. "Choc ice!"

"No, Sarah!" Davey tried to grab it. "It's nasty!"

"Don't interrupt," Molly said crossly. *"I had to fight three Romans with my knife . . ."*

Sarah looked down at the soap and pulled a face. "Nasty!" She gave it to Luke and he began to suck it, like a lollipop.

"No!" Davey shouted.

Molly raised her voice. "*I killed five more Romans . . .*"

But she couldn't go on. Luke was sick all over the rest of her sentence. Very bubbly, soapy sick.

Molly jumped up. "You horrible little boy! I'll have to write it all over again!"

She stamped out of the house, and Davey took the soap away from Luke. "Thanks," he said.

He opened the rag drawer to find something to mop up the sick. There was a worn-out towel, tangled up with old tights and bits of string. He started pulling at it.

Then the phone rang.

"Hallo," said Dad's voice. "Sorry I didn't phone this morning. I was travelling to Paris. And – um – making arrangements. Have you had a good day?"

"Oh *yes!*" Davey said. "We were invaded by Romans, and Molly wanted to thump them. She killed three, but Luke was sick on the rest, and —"

"Hang on!" Dad was laughing so much that Davey could hardly work out what he was saying. "Molly *killed three Romans?*"

"Not *real* Romans!" Davey said. "She – oh, let go, Luke!"

Luke was tugging at an old pair of tights, but it was jumbled up with everything else.

"Legs!" he shouted. "Want legs!"

"Let go!" Davey said. "I'll untangle the legs in a minute."

Dad laughed even louder. It was hard to believe he was so far away. "Who's got tangled legs? Another Roman?"

"Of course not!" said Davey. "It's just –"

And then he had his idea.

The tangled tights *did* look like someone's legs. The legs of someone silly enough to fall into a drawer. Maybe a clumsy idiot who'd tripped over his sword . . .

"Never mind the legs," Dad said, "I've got some news –"

But Davey couldn't think about anything except legs. "Hang on," he said. Putting down the receiver, he pulled all the rags out of the rag drawer. As he ran through the door, he shouted.

"Mum! Dad's on the phone!"

Then he raced upstairs. He was going to make something brilliant. Just for fun.

6. Julius Sneezer

DAVEY SPENT THE rest of the evening
collecting things.

The pyjamas from the rag drawer.

Two old pairs of tights.

A worn out pillow case.

A pile of newspapers.

He'd just piled them up on his
bedroom floor, when Molly opened
the door, without knocking. She
walked straight in.

"I've copied out my story again."
She marched over and sat down on his
bed. Then she saw the heap on the
floor. "What's that rubbish? I'll take it

away. Dad's having a bonfire tomorrow."

"No," Davey said quickly. "I want it."

Molly gave him a suspicious look. "Why? What are you doing? Is it something for the Roman Prize?"

"Of course not. I'm – um – playing dustmen."

"*Dustmen?*" Molly shook her head. "You're *mad*, Davey Tilling. I'll read my story to your mum, instead. *She's* got some sense." She bustled off downstairs.

Davey shut his door tight. Then he began. He stuffed the pillow case with newspaper and tied the end shut, to make a head. Then he stuffed the tights, to make two arms and two legs. He was just going to put them together, inside the pyjamas, when he heard Molly coming back.

Quick as a flash, he threw the whole lot on top of the wardrobe.

Molly sailed in, looking smug. "Your mum says my story's *wonderful*. She said I was a clever little girl. And –" Suddenly, she looked up. Her eyes narrowed. "What are *those*?"

Two fat, brown legs were dangling down from the top of the wardrobe.

"They're – er – for keeping out draughts," Davey gabbled. He tugged at the legs, and they fell on his head. "This one goes round the door." Frantically, he pushed it into place. "And this one goes – um – round the hamster's cage. So he doesn't get a cold. Hamsters hate getting colds. When they sneeze, all the food sprays out of their cheek pouches – WHOOOSH! It goes everywhere, and –"

"You *are* mad," Molly said. "I'm going home."

She shook her head and disappeared. Davey sighed with relief, but he didn't go on with his plan. In case she came back. He felt safer making an assault course for his hamster.

When he got home from school next day, he could hardly wait to get back to the legs.

"We aren't doing anything, are we, Mum?" he said. "I need lots of time."

His mother gave him an odd look. "We're not going *out*. Because we're waiting for —"

"Great!"

Davey didn't wait to hear whom they were waiting for. He headed for the stairs. But, as he reached the bottom, there was a yell.

"Legs!"

Luke and Sarah appeared on the landing with one of his pairs of tights. Clutching one leg each and tugging in opposite directions.

"Let *go!*" Davey said.

There was a horrible, tearing sound. The tights came apart in the middle and Luke and Sarah sat down with a bump. When Davey ran upstairs and grabbed the separate legs, they started to wail.

"My *leg!*"

"Wanta *leg!*"

"Oh, Davey!" said Mum. "How could you make them cry? Just when I'm so busy getting ready for –"

"I'm busy too," Davey said crossly. He went into his bedroom and banged the door.

Using the pyjamas, he managed to make all the bits into a body. Rather a strange body. It was very tall, with a floppy head and long thin legs. Laying

it on the bed, Davey took out his felt
pens.

Carefully, he drew a face on the
pillow case head, trying to make it
look like the Roman soldier at the
fort. With a funny little mouth and
great, bushy eyebrows. And a very big
red nose.

When he'd finished, he took lots of things out of his wardrobe.

The T-shirt, in its blue plastic bag.

The broken piece of wood from the onager.

His brown paper time-line.

The cauldron with the squashed side.

Pulling the T-shirt over the dummy's head, he tied it round the middle with a piece of string. Immediately, the dummy looked more like a soldier in a tunic. Especially when he pinned the plastic bag on to its shoulders, hanging down like a cloak.

The piece of broken wood from the onager made a fine sword. Davey used the rest of his tin of paint to paint it silver and fixed it to the dummy's hand with thick rubber bands.

Uncoiling his time-line, he tore it in half and wound the two brown strips

round the dummy's legs, as sandal straps. It looked even better than he'd hoped, but he wouldn't let himself get excited yet. He picked up the cauldron.

Smoothing the squashed side, he cut it out, in a neat, curved rectangle. He glued a strip of paper to the back, to make a handle, and drew a lightning flash on the silver front. It looked just like the shields in the museum.

All he needed now was a helmet.

He picked up the rest of the cauldron and turned it upside-down, pushing it on to the dummy's head. Then he stepped back to look.

And the tall soldier with the funny face stared back at him, smiling. Just like the soldier at the fort.

"Hallo, Julius Sneezer," Davey said softly.

He was going to call Mum to come and see, but *she* called first.

"Davey! Sarah! Luke! You've got a visitor!"

A visitor? But it was nearly bedtime. Who would come round at a time like that?

There was only one person Davey could think of.

Molly!

7. *Discovered!*

DAVEY GRABBED JULIUS Sneezer and
pushed him into the wardrobe. Then
he opened the door.

Luke and Sarah burst in.

"Come!"

"Come on, Dayee!"

They bumped into him so hard that
he staggered backwards and crashed
into the wardrobe. The doors flew
open, and Julius Sneezer fell out on
top of him. Luke and Sarah shrieked
with delight.

"Man!"

"No!" yelled Davey. He picked the

soldier up and held him out of reach.
Where could he hide him?

"Davey!" Mum sounded impatient.
"Where are you?"

Davey pushed Luke and Sarah
towards the door. "Quick. Mum's got
a nice surprise. Go and see."

They looked doubtful, but they
toddled out and slid down the stairs.
As they went into the kitchen, Davey
heard shrieks of glee. Why were they
so pleased to see Molly?

He didn't have time to find out.
Quickly, he crept across the landing,
into the bathroom. As he bolted the
door, he heard footsteps coming
upstairs. Walking towards his
bedroom. He had to hurry. When
Molly found he wasn't there, she
would start banging on the bathroom
door.

Dragging Julius across the

bathroom, Davey pushed him into the
shower cubicle. He hung him up on
the showerhead and slid the doors
shut.

The feet tiptoed out of his bedroom,
stopped by the bathroom door and
went on, into the twins' room. When
the coast was clear, Davey unbolted

the bathroom door and slipped downstairs.

"Yes, Mum?" he said, innocently. "Did you call?"

Mum looked surprised. "Didn't you see him?"

Davey was listening to the footsteps coming out of the twins' bedroom. Heading for the bathroom. "Him?" he said. "What him?"

Before Mum could answer, there was a noise from upstairs. A laugh.

Suddenly, Davey realized who was up there. It wasn't Molly at all. It was —

"Dad!" he shouted. "Dad! I'm down here!"

He raced out of the kitchen just as a familiar figure appeared at the top of the stairs. A tall man with a funny face and big, bushy eyebrows.

"I think I'm going mad," Dad said,

looking down. "There seems to be an Ancient Roman in the shower."

They all had breakfast together. Luke and Sarah sat on Dad's lap, smearing him with porridge and Marmite, and Davey sat beside him, telling the story of Julius Sneezer. All about the trip to the fort. And what had happened to the onager and the time-line and the cauldron.

And all about Molly.

Dad listened to everything, very quietly. Then he said, "You really wanted to win the Roman Prize, didn't you?"

Davey shrugged. "Well, I can't. We're having our Roman feast tomorrow, and that's when we're choosing the winner. But I haven't got anything to take. I haven't even got any food for the feast."

"What's wrong with taking your soldier?" Dad said.

"*Julius Sneezer?*" Davey stared. "But – Molly would laugh."

Mum sat down on the other side of Davey and began spreading honey on a piece of toast. "Does Molly laugh at you a lot?"

"We-ell." Davey hung his head. "She thinks I'm stupid."

Dad and Mum looked at each other. Then Dad said, "Well, it's time Molly found out she was wrong. *I* think your soldier's wonderful. And I bet all your friends will, too."

Davey thought about Jason and Garry. "They might —"

"That's settled then." Mum held out the piece of toast. "Julius Sneezer's going to school tomorrow."

"But I can't just carry him in. He'd look silly."

Dad took the toast and pushed it into Davey's mouth. "Don't talk. Eat that and listen to me. Julius Sneezer's going to school. *And* you're going to have something very special for the feast . . ."

8. The Roman Feast

NEXT MORNING, MOLLY came round bright and early with a big tin in her hands. And a big grin on her face.

"*I've* got special Ancient Roman food for the feast! My mum's made honey cakes, and stuffed dates and prawn rissoles. *And* marzipan dormice. What have you got?"

"Nothing," said Davey.

"Nothing?" Molly looked shocked. "But we've all got to —"

"My dad's bringing something later," Davey said.

Molly peeped into the house. "What

about the Roman prize? What are you taking for that?"

"Nothing," said Davey.

"*Nothing?*" Molly opened her eyes wide. "*I've* got my onager and my time-line and my twenty-page story."

"Yes," Davey said. "I know." He picked up his coat. "Mum! Molly's here!"

Mum came bustling out of the kitchen, drying her hands. "Let's go then. Thank goodness we haven't got to take the twins. They're upstairs with Dad, eating chocolate biscuits in bed."

Molly looked disapproving. "My mum never lets *me* eat in bed. She says it's too messy."

"You poor little thing," said Davey's mum.

Molly was so surprised that she didn't say another word, all the way to school.

Davey felt very strange that
morning. He was the only person who
hadn't brought anything. Everyone
else was busy getting the feast ready
and arranging models on the display
table. There were three or four
onagers, six time-lines and lots of
swords. Jason and Garry had drawn a
plan of the Roman fort, and Amy had

made a Roman dress for her Sindy
doll.

But no one had made as much as
Molly. She spent the morning looking
smug and pretending to be modest.

"I'm not really the best," she kept
saying. "Everyone else has tried *very
hard*. Amy's Roman dress is lovely.
Even if she has got it wrong. And
Leo's onager is just as good as mine.
Except that it doesn't work."

Davey didn't say a word. But he kept
thinking, *Please don't let Dad forget*.

Dad didn't. At break, as they were
all going into the playground, Davey
saw their big blue car drive past, into
the teachers' car park. He grinned.
But he didn't say a word.

When they went back in after break,
their classroom was ready for the
feast. All the tables were stacked on
one side of the room, and the curtain

was pulled across the end, shutting off the book corner.

Mrs Johnson had made a big low table with the staging from the hall. It was covered with a white cloth, and all the food was spread out on top. Honey cakes and prawn rissoles. Marzipan dormice and stuffed dates. Little brown biscuits, bowls of lentils and boiled eggs with a strange-looking sauce. There was even a big jug of blackcurrant, pretending to be wine.

"We'll lie down to eat," Mrs Johnson said. "That's what the Romans did."

"Yes!" said Jason. "Like eating in bed!"

Molly pulled a face, but no one took any notice. They were too busy looking at the food. Except for Davey. He was staring at the curtain that shut off the book corner. *I hope it's going to be all right*, he thought.

"What about the competition?"
Molly said loudly. "When are we
going to choose the winner?"

"In a minute," Mrs Johnson said.
"But before we vote, there's someone I
want you to see." She smiled at Davey
and marched across to the book
corner. "Meet Julius Sneezer!"

With a flourish, she pulled back
the curtain — and there was Julius,
hanging straight and tall on the
cupboard door, with a biscuit tin at his
feet.

Everyone gasped. Then they started
to laugh and cheer.

"Brilliant!" said Garry.

"Did you make him, Miss?" said
Jason.

"I want him to sit next to *me*," said
Amy.

Mrs Johnson smiled again. "*I* didn't
make him. Davey did. He's been

working on him ever since we went to the Roman fort, haven't you, Davey?"

"Sort of," said Davey. "I —"

He didn't get a chance to explain. Garry spun round and slapped him on the back.

"You're the winner! You've got to be."

Everyone started chanting it. "The winner! The winner!"

The only person not chanting was Molly. She stood by the curtain, glaring at Julius Sneezer. When the shouting died down, she sidled up to Mrs Johnson.

"It's not fair," she said. "*I* thought we had to make the things by ourselves. Davey couldn't have done that on his own. Someone must have helped him."

Mrs Johnson looked at her. "I don't think so, Molly. Davey's father told me

all about it. You didn't have any help, did you, Davey?"

Davey looked at Julius Sneezer. Then he looked at Molly. He had never seen her so miserable and cross.

"I didn't have any *help*," he said slowly. "But I couldn't have done it without –"

Everyone was staring at him, but he was determined to finish.

"I couldn't have done it without *you*, Molly."

Molly went bright scarlet. Suddenly, Davey felt sorry for her. It was a very strange feeling. Bending down, he picked up the biscuit tin that was lying at Julius Sneezer's feet.

"Here," he said. "Have one of these. My dad made them specially for the feast."

He pulled the lid off the tin and Molly peered in suspiciously.

"What are they?"

Davey managed not to smile. "Rhubarb pies," he said.